英韵经典宋诗词百首

Classic Song Poems and Lyrics in English Rhyme

霍红 刘猛 译

中国海洋大学出版社

· 青岛 ·

图书在版编目（CIP）数据

英韵经典宋诗词百首：中英对照／霍红，刘猛译．
青岛：中国海洋大学出版社，2024.12. -- ISBN 978-7-
5670-3889-9

Ⅰ. I222

中国国家版本馆 CIP 数据核字第 20248JM705 号

出版发行	中国海洋大学出版社	
社　　址	青岛市香港东路 23 号	邮政编码　266071
出 版 人	刘文菁	
网　　址	http://pub.ouc.edu.cn	
订购电话	0532-82032573（传真）	
责任编辑	邵成军	电　　话　0532-85902533
印　　制	青岛国彩印刷股份有限公司	
版　　次	2024 年 12 月第 1 版	
印　　次	2024 年 12 月第 1 次印刷	
成品尺寸	170 mm ×230 mm	
印　　张	14	
字　　数	75 千	
印　　数	1—1 000	
定　　价	118.00 元	

译者简介

霍红

　　2001 年成都理工大学英语专业毕业，获文学学士学位；2005 年澳大利亚莫纳什大学国际英语教学专业毕业，获教育学硕士学位；2013 年 12 月至 2014 年 12 月在美国俄克拉何马州立大学英语系访学；2015 年上海外国语大学英语语言文学专业毕业，获博士学位；2015 年 12 月至 2021 年 6 月，于扬州大学文学院做博士后。现为扬州大学外国语学院副教授、硕士生导师。主要学术兴趣包括文学翻译、语用学及二语习得。系江苏省翻译工作者协会会员。主持江苏省教育厅哲学社会科学研究项目 1 项，主持校级科研项目多项，出版教材 2 部，出版《海棠依旧·霍红双语诗集选》自创自译中英双语格律诗著作 1 部，多篇翻译作品在《英语世界》等期刊发表。

The Translator's Profile

Huo Hong, who received a Bachelor's degree in English literature from Chengdu University of Technology in 2001, a Master's degree in TESOL from Monash University, Australia in the December of 2005, a doctoral degree in English language and literature from Shanghai International Studies University in 2015 and who was a visiting scholar to the English Department of Oklahoma State University, the US from the December of 2013 to that of 2014 and was doing postdoctoral research at College of Humanities of Yangzhou University from December, 2015 to June, 2021, is now an associate professor of College of International Studies of Yangzhou University, who supervises postgraduates and whose academic interest covers literary translation, pragmatics and so on. As a member of Jiangsu Translators Association, she is found productive in books and research papers, has undertaken one provincial project funded by Educational Department of Jiangsu Province and was involved in compiling two textbooks. Keen on translating traditional Chinese poems though, she has translated some literary works such as English-translated essays published in *The English World*. More than what relates to her career, she is a poet who has had a poem selection of her own published, namely *Gone and Go On* in both Chinese and English.

译者简介

刘猛

2001 年成都理工大学英语专业毕业，获文学学士学位；2005 年澳大利亚莫纳什大学国际英语教学专业毕业，获教育学硕士学位；2014 年上海外国语大学翻译学专业毕业，获文学博士学位；2015 年 1 月至 2021 年 6 月在扬州大学文学院做博士后；2017 年 8 月至 2018 年 8 月由国家留学基金委员会公派赴美国夏威夷大学教育学院访学。现为扬州大学外国语学院副教授、硕士生导师，江苏省翻译工作者协会理事。主要学术兴趣包括口笔译理论与实践、二语习得。主持教育部专业学位案例库项目 1 项、江苏省教育厅哲学社会科学研究项目 1 项，参与国家社科基金项目 4 项，主持多项校级科研项目，出版教材 6 部，在省级及以上期刊发表学术论文 10 余篇。所指导的学生多次在全国各类英语口笔译比赛中获一等奖。承担各类会议口译、陪同口译 100 余场，笔译工作 200 余万字。

The Translator's Profile

Liu Meng, who received a Bachelor's degree in English literature from Chengdu University of Technology in 2001, a Master's degree in TESOL from Monash University, Australia in 2005, a doctoral degree in interpretation and translation from Shanghai International Studies University in 2014 and who was a visiting scholar to the Department of Education, Hawaii University, the US from the August of 2017 to that of 2018 and was doing postdoctoral research at College of Humanities of Yangzhou University from the January of 2015 to the June of 2021, is now an associate professor of College of International Studies of Yangzhou University, who supervises postgraduates and whose academic interest falls on interpretation and translation and second language teaching. Cast in the multiple role, he is found with a wide range of harvests—having received a grant from China Professional-degree Case Center under Ministry of Education, having completed a Philosophical Science Fund Project granted by Educational Department of Jiangsu Province, being involved in four National Social Science Fund Projects, having been a holder of several university-granted fund projects, textbooks, publications as well as a plurality of awards in teaching or instructing students for interpretation or translation competition. Nonetheless, as a member of Jiangsu Translators Association, he retains his expertise in interpretation and translation by interpreting at a great number of conferences and translating a diversity of works.

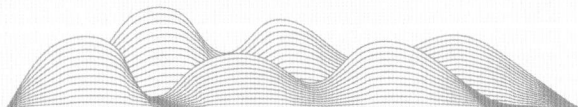

序

　　中国古代诗歌是中华民族的文学瑰宝,以诗和词的形式为人们所熟知。唐诗的璀璨令古代文学达到了顶峰,宋诗的成就虽不如唐诗,却具有自身的特色,尤其是宋代的哲理诗。宋代哲理诗是宋代诗人人生智慧与文学智慧的结晶,是现实主义和浪漫主义的结合,同时也反映了宋代时代大背景下诗人的理性构建。宋代哲理诗往往在说理的同时,注重语言的生动性,令诗人所述的道理在趣味的语言中得以阐明,避免了说教的枯燥。宋诗关注社会现实,关心百姓疾苦,批评统治者的骄奢淫逸,但同时又充满了对美好的憧憬和期待;对自然现象和自然规律的细致观察和体会以及由此进行的联想与感悟,体现了诗人的理性思维。

　　宋词是中国古代文学阆苑中的瑰丽奇葩,在中国古代诗歌史及中国古代文学史上均占有极其重要的地位,其句子长短不一,故而又称为"长短句"。"词"的氛围是孤独,因而其最初以爱情、相思为主要题材,也就难以得到正统文人的青睐。后来,由于白居易、刘禹锡等诗人的关注,词才逐渐成为唐末文人创作的重要体式之一,随之成为被认可的正统文学体式。经过五代时期的发展,到了宋代,词成为主要的文学体式。宋代词人在词上的创作成就达到历代的顶峰,从而成就了"宋词"这一流行在宋代的最擅长抒情、最拨人心弦的文学体式。

　　然而,宋词并未囿于婉约、孤独、怀念等对自身情感的抒发,在创作过程中也逐渐走向对社会的关注,例如苏轼的词大气磅礴、慷慨激昂、情感豪迈,这是词的格局,也是词人的格局,是文学的格局。当词走出自我的小格局,词人便走出了小我,而走向了以政治为背景的大世界,由此词也隔断了其与曲的原始瓜葛,而最终成为独立的文学体式。从此,词分为豪放和婉约两种词风。豪放派词人,苏轼之后有辛弃疾;婉约派词人,有李清照。纵观宋代文人,其创作体式上虽不限于词,然而其在词创作上的成就均远超过其在其他文学体式上的成就。

　　唐诗、宋词和元曲,是中国古代文学发展史上的三座高峰。在中国传统国学复兴的历史时期,它们作为承载中华民族历史、文化与智慧的经典文学形式,应首先得到继承,然后得到发扬,让文化在文学中得以传播。宋代诗人、词人的人生智慧、孤独的情感与豪迈的情怀,均在其文字间隙里得以传达,或有趣,或沉郁,或达观,令人动容,令人沉醉。

　　许渊冲等诗词翻译家从事唐诗宋词的英韵翻译,他们不仅追求还原诗词的"意"之美,也尽量实现"音"与"形"之美,以达到"以诗译诗"的翻译情怀。他们的翻译体式形成了中国古代诗歌翻译的新范式,使其译文与中国古代诗歌全方位无限接近原诗歌,其译文是真正以中国诗词形式呈现的英文译文。"意美""音美"与"形美"是许渊冲提出的诗词的翻译诗学观,致力于令双语在细节上的相似度靠近,是将源语艺术性传递到译文的一种努力。尽管翻译家具有双语极大相似的宏观愿景,却由于宋词中辞藻的复杂、语法不规则等因素,已有的宋诗词英韵译文出现诸多与原诗词较远的背向,因而令译文失去了原文的等值意美与艺术通感。

　　"如果同一文本存在两个或更多的相同译入语译文,新译文往往比早期出现的译文更加接近原文"(Paloposki & Koskinen 2004)。对国学经典翻译的精益求精是后来翻译者的向往与追求,翻译者对译诗无限接近原诗的孜孜不倦的探索是国学经典对外传播的动力。赵彦春教授的《英韵宋词百首》正体现了这样孜孜以求地探寻更佳译诗的精神和努力。本书作者同样秉承着这样的精神，也做着与前辈们相似的努力。

　　本书获得中国海洋大学出版社邵成军主任的大力支持以及扬州大学出版基金资助，特此感谢。

霍 红　刘 猛

2024 年 5 月 1 日于扬州

英韵经典宋诗词百首

Preface

The Chinese ancient poetry is the literary treasure in the recognized forms of poetry and lyrics. Song poems, unable to compare with Tang poems, which reached the peak of the Chinese ancient literature, have some unique characteristics of their own, particularly the philosophical poems. Philosophical poems of the Song Dynasty are the fruit of life wisdom and literary wisdom, a marriage of realism and romanticism, and a reflection of constructing reason in the background of the Song Dynasty. As they attempt to reason out a truth, Song philosophical poems tend to have some delightful quality in order that life truths can be elicited in the style of amusing language, monotony avoided in reasoning. Attending to social reality and the sufferings of the people, Song philosophical poems, with the aim to condemn the ruler's dissipated life, involve longings for good life and great expectations. Through meticulous observation, personal experience, mental connections and active perception, Song philosophical poems embody the poet's mindset of reason.

Song lyrics, believed as a miracle in Chinese ancient literature, have played a major role in the history of the Chinese ancient poetry and literature, also termed as "long and short sentences" owing to their differed lengths in different lines. The atmosphere that lyrics create is prone to loneliness, which leads them to the conveyance of romantics and lovesickness, thereby disfavoured by orthodox literati at first. Afterwards, Bai Juyi and Liu Yuxi's attention paid to this fashion of literature, lyrics came to be recognized as a major literary model adopted by literati of the late Tang Dynasty, known as a widely recognized literary model. Evolving through the Five Dynasties, lyrics have become the leading literary model of the Song Dynasty. The number and quality of lyrics composed by poets of the Song Dynasty have achieved a peak throughout all the dynasties, which leads to Song lyrics being the most lyrical, the most heart-stirring literary model prevailing in the Song Dynasty.

However, Song lyrics not merely aim at voicing one's graceful restraint, loneliness and old things or people recalling but also change to the attention to society in the course of composing lyrics, such as Su Shi's lyrics of grandeur, vehemence, and boldness, which reflect a wide vision of poems, that of the lyric composers and that of literature composition. When lyrics get out of the lyric composer's constraint, the composers step out of their constrained selves to the bigger world of a political background, which thus cuts off lyrics' in-born connection with music and makes them an independent literary model. From then on, lyrics fall into two categories, unconstrained school and restrained school. Most typical of unconstrained school is Xin Qiji that comes after Su Shi and most typical of restrained school is Li Qingzhao that comes also after Su Shi. Overviewed throughout, all literati of the Song Dynasty whose literary composing model did not fall within the limit of lyrics have achieved better in lyric writing than in other literary composing models.

Tang poems, Song lyrics and Yuan songs are the three literary peaks in the history of Chinese ancient literature. In the time of the renaissance experienced by the traditional Chinese studies, the three literary models, which are classic literary forms bearing the Chinese history, culture and wisdom, should be inherited and carried forward, with the Chinese culture to spread home and abroad by means of literary works. Life wisdom, loneliness and vehemence of the poets and lyric composers of the Song Dynasty are conveyed in and between the lines, which are either amusing, or gloomy, or philosophically optimistic to stir the reader's heart and captivate his soul.

Translators such as Xu Yuanchong engage in metrical translation of Song lyrics in English rhyme, aiming not only at restoring the "Message Beauty" in the English-translated lyric but also at achieving the "Prosodic Beauty" and the

"Image Beauty" to realize their aspiration for "the poetic translation", whose translation model has made a new epoch in Chinese ancient poem, lyric and song translation, rendering the translated works infinitely close to the original texts. This version of translated work in the true sense showcases itself in the shape of the Chinese ancient poems, lyrics and songs. The "Triple Beauty" theory in poetic translation put forward by Xu Yuanchong covers "Message Beauty", "Prosodic Beauty" and "Image Beauty", the three of which are applied to bring the original texts and the translated works more alike to each other and are a representation of the translator's effort to transport the artistic quality of the original texts into the translated works. Macroscopic as translator's ambition is in bringing what's in the original text into the translated texts, the existing metrically translated Tang poems and Song lyrics are found a distance away from the original texts, the art in them and empathy lost, on account of the sophistication of language, unconstrained use of grammar and so on in the original texts.

As Paloposki and Koskinen (2004) believe, the later translation tends to get closer to the original text than the earlier one if there are two or more versions of the original text translated into the same language. Better translation of the Chinese ancient classics is the pursuit of subsequent translators, whose assiduous effort to seek a closer version of translation is the engine for the spread of Chinese classics to the West. *Tang Poems in English Rhyme* by Professor Zhao Yanchun showcases such assiduity and persistence for better translated poems. Bearing such an ambition, we are following in the way of those vanguards.

With greatest sincerity, we herein extend our gratitude to Shao Chengjun, executive editor of China Ocean University Press for his affirmation and to Yangzhou University for the Publishing Grant.

Huo Hong & Liu Meng
May 1st, 2024 in Yangzhou

英韵经典宋诗词百首

目录 CONTENTS

· 宋诗 Song Poems ·

英韵经典宋诗词百首

• 宋词 Song Lyrics •

3

目录

·参考文献·

宋 诗
Song Poems

江上渔者

范仲淹

江上往来人，
但爱鲈鱼美。
君看一叶舟，
出没风波里。

Fishermen on the River

Fan Zhongyan

Those who come to the River or above,
The delicacy of perch they do love.
Lo and behold, there flows a small small boat,
Up and down between waves it stays afloat.

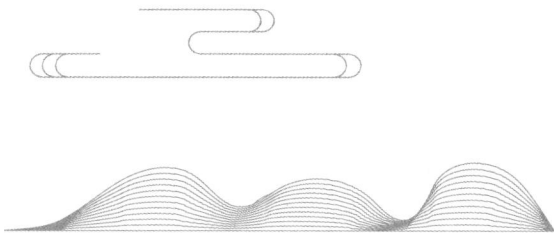

泊船瓜洲

王安石

京口瓜洲一水间，
钟山只隔数重山。
春风又绿江南岸，
明月何时照我还。

Mooring at Guazhou

Wang Anshi

Jingkou's a River across from Guazhou;
Mt. Zhong sits just a few mountains away.
Greening th' River's south again, spring winds blow;
When will the moon see me back on my way?

元 日

王安石

爆竹声中一岁除，
春风送暖入屠苏。
千门万户曈曈日，
总把新桃换旧符。

The Chinese New Year's Day

Wang Anshi

Amid cracks of fireworks, a year does end;
Tusu wine drunk, warmth the spring wind does send.
Upon gates and windows the sun does shine;
Old peach wood charms are changed to the new sign.

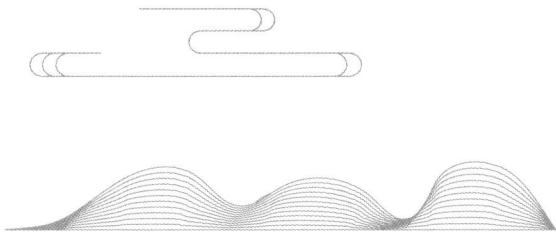

梅 花

王安石

墙角数枝梅，
凌寒独自开。
遥知不是雪，
为有暗香来。

The Wintersweet
Wang Anshi

In the wall corner some twigs loom,
On which plum blossoms in th' cold bloom.
You know afar snow they can't be,
'Cause subtle sweetness reaches me.

书湖阴先生壁

王安石

茅檐长扫净无苔，
花木成畦手自栽。
一水护田将绿绕，
两山排闼送青来。

The Inscription on the Wall of Mr. Huyin

Wang Anshi

Swept oft neath th' thatched eaves, it's mossless and clean;
Grass and trees in line, grown there they have been.
A moat defends and circles the field green;
The two hills open, the green in between.

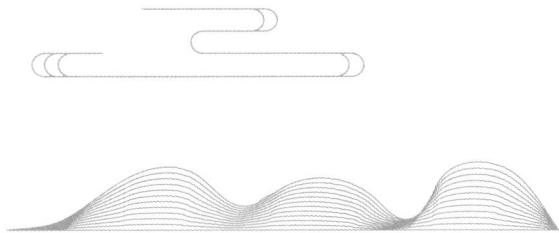

登飞来峰

王安石

飞来山上千寻塔，
闻说鸡鸣见日升。
不畏浮云遮望眼，
自缘身在最高层。

Ascending the Winged Peak

Wang Anshi

On th' Winged Peak the pagoda's to the sky;
As said, cocks' crows bring sunrise to the eye.
Do not fear the floating clouds veil your sight;
For you are at the very utmost height.

春日偶成

程 颢

云淡风轻近午天，
傍花随柳过前川。
时人不识余心乐，
将谓偷闲学少年。

An Improvised Poem on a Spring Day

Cheng Hao

To midday with light clouds and gentle breeze,
I pass th' stream along blooms and willow trees.
Those who do not know the pleasure of mine
Would say I'm like youths to spare time for ease.

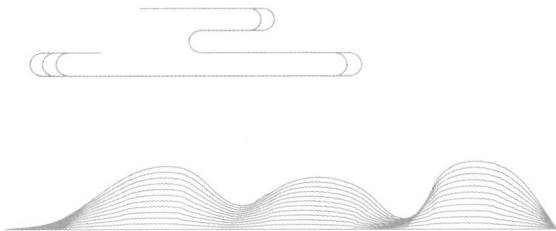

秋日偶成

程 颢

闲来无事不从容，
睡觉东窗日已红。
万物静观皆自得，
四时佳兴与人同。
道通天地有形外，
思入风云变态中。
富贵不淫贫贱乐，
男儿到此是豪雄。

An Improvised Poem on an Autumn Day

Cheng Hao

At leisure, with none without ease I deal;
As I wake at morn, th' east window's been red.
Viewed close, everything gives an easy feel;
To th' same interest four seasons' scenes have led.
All truths go beyond th' tangible on earth;
Thoughts seep in changes of cloud's and wind's form.
Rich, be not loose, and deprived, stay with mirth.
Heroes are men up to the above norm.

题西林壁

苏 轼

横看成岭侧成峰，
远近高低各不同。
不识庐山真面目，
只缘身在此山中。

An Inscription on Westwood Wall

Su Shi

A ridge seen afront and a peak aside,
Different seen from high or low, near or far,
Mt. Lu with its true self cannot be eyed,
Because it's in the mountain that you are.

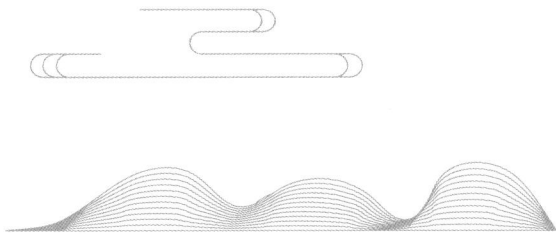

琴 诗

苏 轼

若言琴上有琴声，
放在匣中何不鸣？
若言声在指头上，
何不于君指上听？

A Poem on Guqin①

Su Shi

If in Guqin music exists,
Why in the case are strings not stirred?
If through fingers music consists,
Why from fingers is it not heard?

---

① Guqin, a seven-stringed plucked instrument similar to a zither.

饮湖上初晴后雨

苏 轼

水光潋滟晴方好，
山色空蒙雨亦奇。
欲把西湖比西子，
淡妆浓抹总相宜。

A Drink by West Lake from Fine to Rainy

Su Shi

Glitters of water in th' sun bright,
Mist over hills in the rain right,
To Xi Shi, West Lake I compare;
Makeup light or heavy, she's fair.

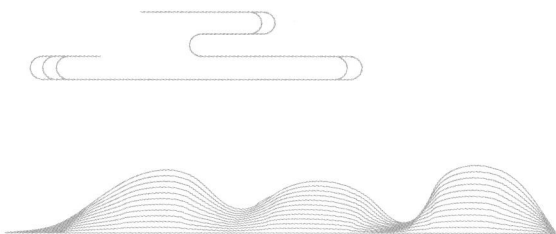

赠刘景文

苏 轼

荷尽已无擎雨盖，
菊残犹有傲霜枝。
一年好景君须记，
最是橙黄橘绿时。

To Liu Jingwen

Su Shi

The lotus dead, the lily pads are gone,
Withered in frost mums proud stalks still stand on.
Remember the best time of year it's been;
Oranges turn yellow, tangerines green.

六月二十七日望湖楼醉书

苏 轼

黑云翻墨未遮山，
白雨跳珠乱入船。
卷地风来忽吹散，
望湖楼下水如天。

Drunk Writing at the Lake
Watching Tower on 27th Day of the Sixth Moon

Su Shi

In ink-made clouds hides no hill top;
Into the boat romps the rain drop.
With wind twirls, away the clouds fly;
At th' tower, water mirrors th' sky.

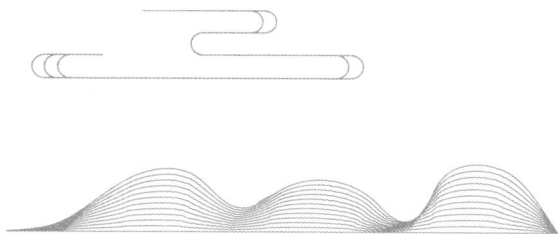

惠崇春江晚景

苏 轼

竹外桃花三两枝，
春江水暖鸭先知。
蒌蒿满地芦芽短，
正是河豚欲上时。

A Twilight View of the Spring River Drawn by Huichong

Su Shi

Beyond th' bamboo, two or three peach twigs show;
Spring rills get warm, ducks are the first to know.
Wormwood all over the ground, reed shoots low,
It's time that globefish went up the stream flow.

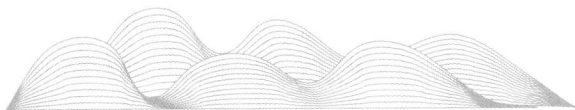

秋日（其二）

秦 观

月团新碾瀹花瓷，
饮罢呼儿课楚词。
风定小轩无落叶，
青虫相对吐秋丝。

A Day in Fall (No. 2)

Qin Guan

I broke th' tea cake, made tea in th' china cup,
'Nd bade my son learn th' Chu Songs when drinking up.
There's no wind or fallen leaves in the yard;
A few worms are spinning silk of fall hard.

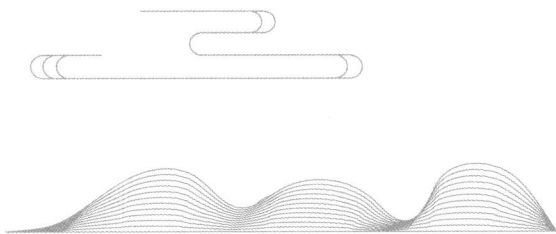

夏日绝句

李清照

生当作人杰，
死亦为鬼雄。
至今思项羽，
不肯过江东。

A Quatrain Composed in Summer

Li Qingzhao

Alive, be a hero mid men;
Dead, be a great one mid ghosts then.
We still miss Xiang Yu up to now;
Not to cross th' River he did vow.

三衢道中

曾 几

梅子黄时日日晴，
小溪泛尽却山行。
绿阴不减来时路，
添得黄鹂四五声。

On the Way to Sanqu

Zeng Ji

As plums turn yellow, it is bright each day;
At th' end of th' stream, th' hill way I take.
Th' green shade's no less than that of th' coming way,
More than that, here's some sound that orioles make.

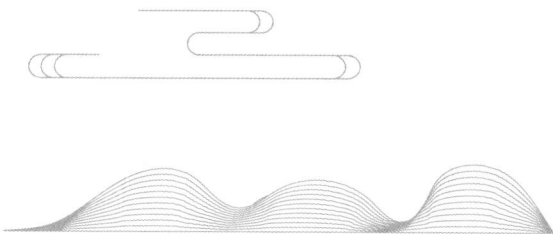

游山西村

陆 游

莫笑农家腊酒浑，
丰年留客足鸡豚。
山重水复疑无路，
柳暗花明又一村。
箫鼓追随春社近，
衣冠简朴古风存。
从今若许闲乘月，
拄杖无时夜叩门。

A Tour of a Village West of the Hills

Lu You

Don't laugh at th' unstrained lunar-twelfth-month self-brewed wine;

You treat me to chicken and pork in th' good-yield years.

Endless hills 'nd rills cause a doubt on th' way out of mine;

Willows green, blooms bright, another village appears.

Flutes and drums to ears, Spring Sacrifice Day to dawn,

With clothes and hat plain, ancient customs remain.

If I can ride th' moonlight at leisure from now on;

I'll come 'nd knock anytime at your door with my cane.

示 儿

陆 游

死去元知万事空，
但悲不见九州同。
王师北定中原日，
家祭无忘告乃翁。

To My Sons

Lu You

Once gone, one knows he owns all things in vain;
Not seeing th' country unified, I'm sad.
When Song Troops go north 'nd have back th' Central Plain,
Sweeping tombs, don't forget to tell your dad.

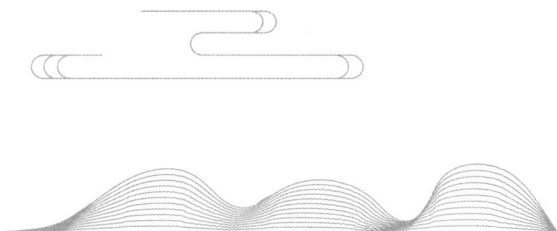

秋夜将晓出篱门迎凉有感

陆　游

三万里河东入海，
五千仞岳上摩天。
遗民泪尽胡尘里，
南望王师又一年。

An Autumn Night Thought
at the Chill Out of the Wood Door

Lu You

Thirty thousand miles east to th' sea th' ri'er flies;
Th' mountain rises five thousand feet to th' skies.
At Hu's area ends th' loyal Han folks' tear;
They expect th' royal troops year after year.

冬夜读书示子聿

陆　游

古人学问无遗力，
少壮工夫老始成。
纸上得来终觉浅，
绝知此事要躬行。

An Instruction to Ziyu
on Reading on a Winter Night

Lu You

No toil spared, knowledge past scholars acquire;
With work in youth, when old you will achieve.
What is from books is light, you will perceive;
For a full knowledge, practice you require.

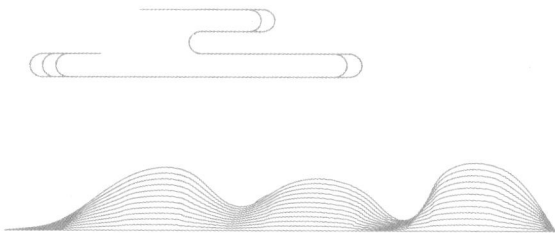

一壶歌

陆 游

长安市上醉春风，
乱插繁花满帽红。
看尽人间兴废事，
不曾富贵不曾穷。

Song of a Wine Pot

Lu You

Along Chang'an streets, drunk in the spring breeze,
Blooms on head, I witness a red-hat scene.
All the ups and downs in the world one sees,
Well-to-do or deprived he has not been.

四时田园杂兴（其二十五）

范成大

梅子金黄杏子肥，
麦花雪白菜花稀。
日长篱落无人过，
惟有蜻蜓蛱蝶飞。

An Impromptu on Countryside Life (No. 25)

Fan Chengda

Plums turn golden and ripe apricots grow,
Rape flowers few, buckwheat blooms white like snow.
Th' day long, fence low with no one going by,
Only dragonflies and butterflies fly.

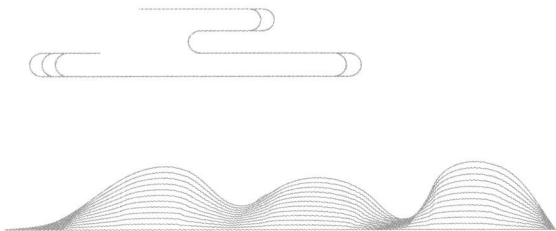

四时田园杂兴（其三十一）

范成大

昼出耘田夜绩麻，
村庄儿女各当家。
童孙未解供耕织，
也傍桑阴学种瓜。

An Impromptu on Countryside Life (No. 31)

Fan Chengda

Weeding fields by day 'nd twisting hemp by night,
Men 'nd women in th' village get their jobs right.
How to till land or weave children don't know;
In th' mulberry shade, gourds they learn to sow.

小 池

杨万里

泉眼无声惜细流，
树阴照水爱晴柔。
小荷才露尖尖角，
早有蜻蜓立上头。

The Small Pond

Yang Wanli

A silent spring mouth spares its trickling flow;
Th' tree shade in water loves mild sunny blow.
The lotus bud shows just a pointed top;
A dragonfly's already stood atop.

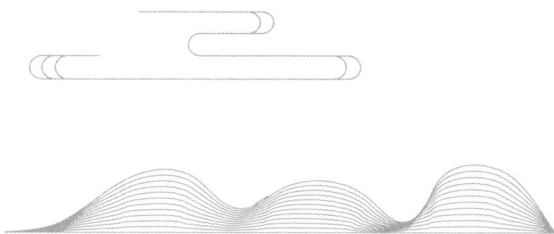

英韵经典宋诗词百首

晓出净慈寺送林子方

杨万里

毕竟西湖六月中，
风光不与四时同。
接天莲叶无穷碧，
映日荷花别样红。

Seeing Off Lin Zifang
Out of Jingci Temple at Daybreak

Yang Wanli

After all it is the mid-June West Lake;
Distinct from that of other times is th' sight.
A way to th' sky th' endless lily pads make;
Th' lotus in th' sun is red, uniquely bright.

桂源铺

杨万里

万山不许一溪奔，
拦得溪声日夜喧。
到得前头山脚尽，
堂堂溪水出前村。

A Poem Composed
at Guiyuan Courier Station

Yang Wanli

Myriad mountains don't allow th' stream to flow;
The block leads the stream to night-and-day roars.
Till the end of the mountains it does go;
Out the village in front the grand stream pours.

过松源晨炊漆公店（其五）

杨万里

莫言下岭便无难，
赚得行人错喜欢。
政入万山圈子里，
一山放出一山拦。

Cooking in the Morning
at Qigong Inn when Passing Songyuan (No. 5)

Yang Wanli

It's not hard to climb down the ridge, say not,
Which leads passers to a liking in vain.
In the forest of mountains you have got;
One lets you go and one blocks you again.

春 日

朱 熹

胜日寻芳泗水滨，
无边光景一时新。
等闲识得东风面，
万紫千红总是春。

A Spring Day

Zhu Xi

One fine day, I'm for the Si River's spring,
To th' endless land, a new look it does bring.
To east winds people get to be alive;
Always mid purple 'nd red, spring does arrive.

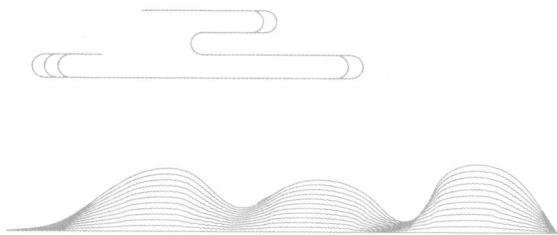

观书有感

朱　熹

半亩方塘一鉴开，
天光云影共徘徊。
问渠那得清如许？
为有源头活水来。

Getting Inspired by Reading

Zhu Xi

A mirror opens half-an-acre pond square;

Th' sky glow and clouds are cast, lingering there.

Why on earth can th' pond water be so clear?

Because th' flowing water from th' source comes here.

活水亭观书有感

朱 熹

昨夜江边春水生，
艨艟巨舰一毛轻。
向来枉费推移力，
此日中流自在行。

Getting Inspired by Reading at Living Water Pavilion

Zhu Xi

The spring river rises last night;
The large warship is feather-light.
It has always been pushed in vain;
Now it goes midstream with no strain.

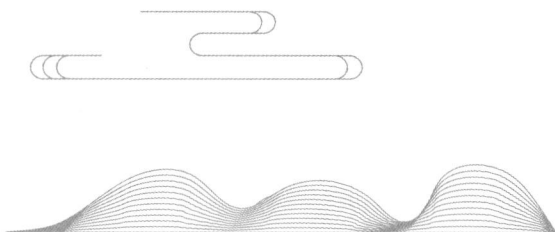

乡村四月

翁 卷

绿遍山原白满川，
子规声里雨如烟。
乡村四月闲人少，
才了蚕桑又插田。

The Fourth Moon of the Country

Weng Juan

Green all over hills 'nd plains, rills white in hue,
Mid cuckoos' trills, rain falls a misty view.
Country of the fourth moon sees idlers few;
After sericulture sowing is due.

题临安邸

林 升

山外青山楼外楼，
西湖歌舞几时休？
暖风熏得游人醉，
直把杭州作汴州。

An Inscription
on the Wall of Lin'an Inn

Lin Sheng

Beyond mountains and towers, they extend;
When on earth will song 'nd dance at West Lake end?
Strollers become drunk with warm winds that blow,
Who have mistaken Hangzhou as Bianzhou.

约 客

赵师秀

黄梅时节家家雨，
青草池塘处处蛙。
有约不来过夜半，
闲敲棋子落灯花。

In Wait for a Guest

Zhao Shixiu

Rain falls from house to house as plums go red;
Everywhere amid ponds and grass frogs spread.
The guest fails to come even past mid night;
Tapping chess pieces drops th' wick, my heart light.

春有百花秋有月

慧 开

春有百花秋有月，
夏有凉风冬有雪。
莫将闲事挂心头，
便是人间好时节。

In Spring Flowers Bloom
and in Fall Moonlight Flows

Monk Huikai

In spring flowers bloom 'nd in fall moonlight flows;
In summer th' breeze blows 'nd in winter it snows.
Don't have on your mind the concerns unworth;
Then you would be at the best time on earth.

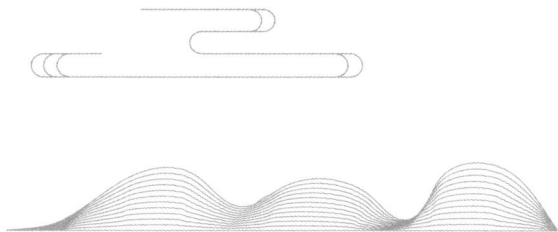

游园不值

叶绍翁

应怜屐齿印苍苔，
小扣柴扉久不开。
春色满园关不住，
一枝红杏出墙来。

An Unreceived Visit to a Garden

Ye Shaoweng

For fear that my sabots are printed on the moss,
Despite my knocks, th' wood gate doesn't let me across.
A gardenful of spring colours walls cannot hold;
Out of the wall an apricot twig does unfold.

夜书所见

叶绍翁

萧萧梧叶送寒声，
江上秋风动客情。
知有儿童挑促织，
夜深篱落一灯明。

On What Was Seen at Night

Ye Shaoweng

Phoenix tree leaves sough a sough, sending chill.
Autumn winds o'er th' River let my thought spill.
I guess that with crickets my children play,
Deep at night by th' fence while a lamp does ray.

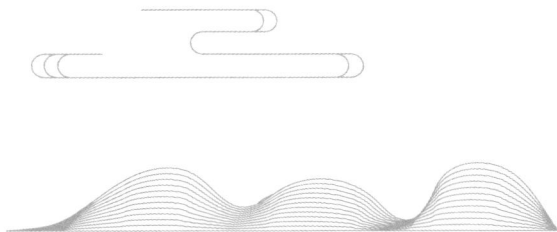

雪梅（其一）

卢梅坡

梅雪争春未肯降，
骚人阁笔费评章。
梅须逊雪三分白，
雪却输梅一段香。

Snow and Plum Blossoms (No. 1)

Lu Meipo

Plum blossoms 'nd snow in spring for no defeat,
Poets put down brushes, comments hard to write.
Snow outshines plum blossoms in being white;
Plum blossoms outdoes snow in being sweet.

雪梅（其二）

卢梅坡

有梅无雪不精神，
有雪无诗俗了人。
日暮诗成天又雪，
与梅并作十分春。

Snow and Plum Blossoms (No. 2)

Lu Meipo

Plum blossoms lifeless without snow,
With no poem snow remains so-so.
With poems done at dusk, it re-snows;
With plum blossoms the right spring shows.

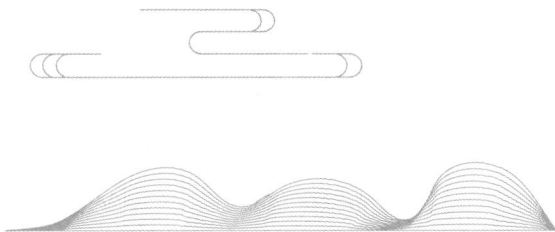

宋 词
Song Lyrics

江南春

寇 准

波渺渺，
柳依依。
孤村芳草远，
斜日杏花飞。
江南春尽离肠断，
蘋满汀洲人未归。

Spring of the South

Kou Zhun

Mist 'nd waves don't end;
Willows sway 'nd bend.
Far grass of the lonely village does lie;
High in th' slanting sun apricot blooms fly.
Spring gone from the South, with woe my heart's burned.
Clover ferns o'er th' shoal, he hasn't returned.

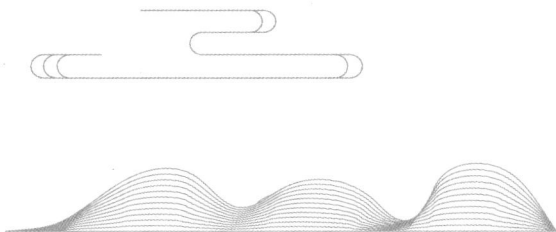

长相思·吴山青

林 逋

吴山青。
越山青。
两岸青山相对迎。
谁知离别情。

君泪盈。
妾泪盈。
罗带同心结未成。
江边潮已平。

Long Longing·Wu Mountains Green

Lin Bu

Wu Mountains green,
Yue mountains green,
Green mountains with a river in between,
Aware of th' parting woe who's been?

Tears fill your eyes,
Tears fill my eyes,
And the silk girdle made into no ties,
To the riverside the rides rise.

雨霖铃

柳 永

寒蝉凄切。
对长亭晚,
骤雨初歇。
都门帐饮无绪,
留恋处、
兰舟催发。
执手相看泪眼,
竟无语凝噎。
念去去、
千里烟波,
暮霭沉沉楚天阔。

多情自古伤离别。
更那堪、
冷落清秋节!
今宵酒醒何处?
杨柳岸、
晓风残月。
此去经年,
应是良辰好景虚设。
便纵有千种风情,
更与何人说?

Bells Ringing in the Rain

Liu Yong

Woe cicada chirps send.
At th' dusk pavilion late,
A sudden pour does end.
I have no mood to have wine by the gate,
Lingering with no bye,
I was rushed to depart.
We hold hands, eyes on th' other, tears in th' eye,
Sobbing, saying no words of heart.
Now I will go,
Over miles of wave flow,
Under vast southern skies and dusk clouds low.

Those in love grieve at parting from of old.
Besides what's there,
In the time of autumn so cold,
Drunk, I wake not knowing it's where;
On th' bank is th' willow tree,
Under the waning moon in the morn air.
For some years it will be,
Times good 'nd fine
'Nd best scenes in vain.
Despite romance of mine,
With whom I'll share what's in mind lain?

蝶恋花

柳 永

伫倚危楼风细细，
望极春愁，
黯黯生天际。
草色烟光残照里，
无言谁会凭阑意？

拟把疏狂图一醉，
对酒当歌，
强乐还无味。
衣带渐宽终不悔，
为伊消得人憔悴。

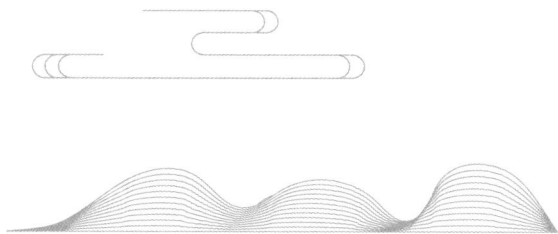

The Butterfly in Love with Blooms

Liu Yong

I lean against th' tower rail in th' light breeze;
As far as the eye sees,
The spring woe rises from th' far sky.
In th' grass-tinged setting sun smoke rises high;
I'm mute against th' rail—who understands why?

To render myself wholly drunk I meant;
To sing with wine I went,
Dry is being forced to be gay.
For reduced girth, unregretful I stay;
For you I would so like to pine away.

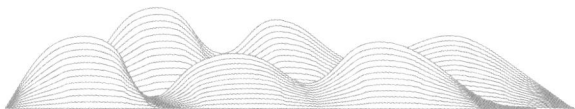

渔家傲·秋思

范仲淹

塞下秋来风景异，
衡阳雁去无留意。
四面边声连角起，
千嶂里，
长烟落日孤城闭。

浊酒一杯家万里，
燕然未勒归无计。
羌管悠悠霜满地，
人不寐，
将军白发征夫泪。

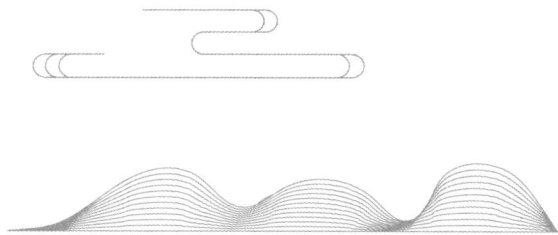

Fishermen's Pride·An Autumn Thought

Fan Zhongyan

As autumn comes, a strange scene th' frontier shows;
Meaning not to stay, wild geese are south-bound.
An uproar from all sides, therewith th' horn blows;
Peaks rise around;
Gate closed, over th' lone town th' sun sets 'nd smoke goes.

A cup of wine drunk, home lies far away;
Border unwon, to go home I don't plan.
With the flute, over the ground frost does stay;
Sleep no one can;
Soldiers to tears, General's hair turns grey.

苏幕遮

范仲淹

碧云天，
黄叶地。
秋色连波，
波上寒烟翠。
山映斜阳天接水。
芳草无情，
更在斜阳外。

黯乡魂，
追旅思。
夜夜除非，
好梦留人睡。
明月楼高休独倚。
酒入愁肠，
化作相思泪。

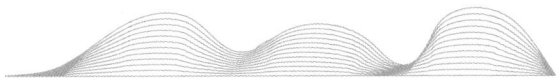

Sumuzhe Dance

Fan Zhongyan

Clouds float, th' sky blue,

Brown leaves allwhere;

Waves steeped in th' autumn hue.

Green are waves in th' cold misty air.

Hills in the setting sun, to skies th' wave flows.

The green grass does not care;

Beyond th' slanting sunlight it grows.

Th' homesick heart right

Lost in thought deep,

Unless each 'nd every night,

Good dreams lull me into good sleep.

Don't lean alone on th' rail on which th' moon veers.

In th' sad heart th' wine does seep,

Transformed into nostalgic tears.

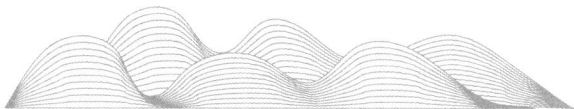

千秋岁

张　先

数声鶗鴂。
又报芳菲歇。
惜春更把残红折。
雨轻风色暴，
梅子青时节。
永丰柳，
无人尽日飞花雪。

莫把幺弦拨。
怨极弦能说。
天不老，
情难绝。
心似双丝网，
中有千千结。
夜过也，
东窗未白凝残月。

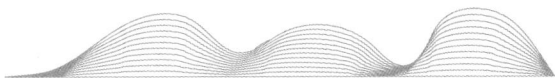

A Thousand Years

Zhang Xian

Several cuckoos sing,

Which again tells the end of spring.

To cherish spring, do snap the withered red.

Rain light, hither fierce wind does head;

It's the season that plums are green.

The willows seen,

None around, catkins fly all day—th' snow scene.

Do you not pluck the finest string;

The utmost woe out it can't bring.

Heaven not old,

Love hard to w'thhold,

A heart's like the double-wired net,

In which thousands of knots are set.

Past is the night;

The waning moon hangs, th' east window not white.

菩萨蛮

张　先

玉人又是匆匆去。
马蹄何处垂杨路。
残日倚楼时，
断魂郎未知。

阑干移倚遍。
薄幸教人怨。
明月却多情。
随人处处行。

The Buddha Envoy

Zhang Xian

Away my dearest he hastily gets;
Where on th' willow-lined lane does his steed go?
I lean on th' rail when the sun sets;
My heart breaks, which he does not know.

From rail to rail, on all I lean;
His heartlessness puts me in woe.
Amorous the moon but has been;
It's with me wherever I go.

诉衷情

张　先

花前月下暂相逢。
苦恨阻从容。
何况酒醒梦断，
花谢月朦胧。

花不尽，
月无穷。
两心同。
此时愿作，
杨柳千丝，
绊惹春风。

Telling the Innermost Feelings

Zhang Xian

Before blooms, under th' moon, we briefly met;
Not to take my time I regret.
What's more, I wake from wine 'nd dreams end;
Blooms fall, dim light for th' moon to send.

Flowers to bloom,
The moon to loom,
Our hearts the same,
Now I wish I became
Th' willow's string upon string
To keep the breeze of spring.

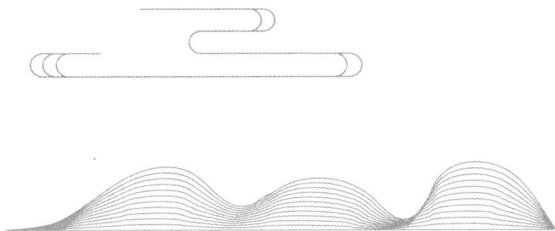

浣溪沙

晏 殊

一曲新词酒一杯。
去年天气旧亭台。
夕阳西下几时回。

无可奈何花落去，
似曾相识燕归来。
小园香径独徘徊。

Yarn Washing

Yan Shu

A new lyric a cup of wine has met,
Last year's weather and pavilion to get.
When does the sun come back up that has set?

To accept the fall of blooms I'm not prone.
Back the swallow I vaguely know has flown.
I pace up and down the fragrant path alone.

浣溪沙

晏 殊

一向年光有限身。
等闲离别易销魂。
酒筵歌席莫辞频。

满目山河空念远，
落花风雨更伤春。
不如怜取眼前人。

Yarn Washing

Yan Shu

Time goes by and one has a short life span,
Partings prone to break the heart of a man.
Banquets or feasts with th' songstress you don't ban.

Hills and rills in sight, missed is the far he;
Sad for fallen blooms in wind 'nd rain I'll be.
I'd best dote on the one in front of me.

清平乐

晏 殊

红笺小字。
说尽平生意。
鸿雁在云鱼在水。
惆怅此情难寄。

斜阳独倚西楼。
遥山恰对帘钩。
人面不知何处，
绿波依旧东流。

The Pure Serene Tune

Yan Shu

Writing's on paper red,
Where all my love for you does spread.
Wild geese over clouds, in water fish wend.
My melancholy's hard to send.

When th' sun sets, on th' tower alone I lean.
Opposite th' curtain th' far hill's been.
Who knows where my pretty looks go?
Green waves still go on an east flow.

玉楼春·春景

宋 祁

东城渐觉风光好。

縠皱波纹迎客棹。

绿杨烟外晓寒轻,

红杏枝头春意闹。

浮生长恨欢娱少。

肯爱千金轻一笑。

为君持酒劝斜阳,

且向花间留晚照。

Jade Tower in Spring·A Spring Scene

Song Qi

Scenery's better east of town;

Ripples to guests and boats roll down.

In the dawn mist, green willows sway;

Spring's in apricot blossom spray.

Grief on little joy all the while,

He won't spare ingots for a smile.

I raise my cup for th' setting sun;

On the blossoms the sun rays run.

鹧鸪天

宋 祁

画毂雕鞍狭路逢。
一声肠断绣帘中。
身无彩凤双飞翼，
心有灵犀一点通。

金作屋，玉为笼。
车如流水马游龙。
刘郎已恨蓬山远，
更隔蓬山几万重。

The Partridge in the Sky

Song Qi

On a path her pleasure cart I speed by.
Behind th' curtain comes a heart-breaking cry.
With no wings of th' phoenix, we fly a pair;
With telepathy, we connect a share.

The room of gold, th' cage of jade rim,
Carts like water flow 'nd steeds like loongs to swim,
The man sighs: celestial mountains are far;
Between us a myriad of mountains are.

生查子·情景

姚 宽

郎如陌上尘,
妾似堤边絮。
相见两悠扬,
踪迹无寻处。

酒面扑春风,
泪眼零秋雨。
过了离别时,
还解相思否?

The Green Haw·The Scene That Stirs My Heart

Yao Kuan

You are like dust o'er where lanes lie;
I'm like th' catkin over the shore.
We meet and apart we soon fly;
Your trace can't be found anymore.

On spring wind a drunk face does dart;
Like autumn rain tears of mine flow.
After the moment when we part,
My lovesickness do you yet know?

生查子·元夕

欧阳修

去年元夜时，
花市灯如昼。
月上柳梢头，
人约黄昏后。

今年元夜时，
月与灯依旧。
不见去年人，
泪湿春衫袖。

The Green Haw·Lantern Festival

Ouyang Xiu

Last year's Lantern Festival night,
The lanterns lit market day-bright.
Over the willow th' moon climbed high;
We'd tryst under the dusky sky.

Lantern Festival night this year,
The moon and lanterns remain here.
Th' one here last I no more retrieve;
Tears have wetted my youth-time sleeve.

浪淘沙·今日北池游

欧阳修

今日北池游。
漾漾轻舟。
波光潋滟柳条柔。
如此春来春又去，
白了人头。

好妓好歌喉。
不醉难休。
劝君满满酌金瓯。
纵使花时常病酒，
也是风流。

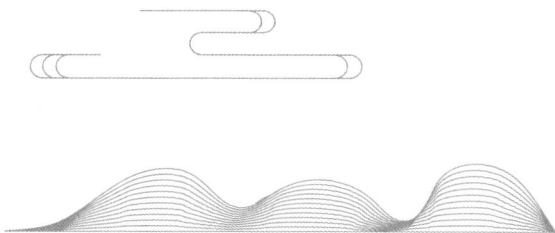

Waves Washing Sand·We Tour North Pond Today

Ouyang Xiu

We tour North Pond today.
Mid waves boats flow.
The ripples shimmer, and soft wickers grow.
Like this, spring again does come and then go.
One's hair turns gray.

At th' singing girl 'nd her voice,
Let's drink, drunk up.
My dear friend, fill and refill your gold cup.
Though mid blooms we have too many a sup.
It's to rejoice.

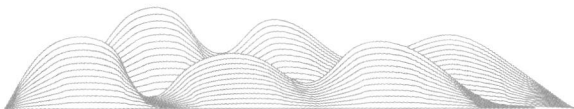

采桑子·轻舟短棹西湖好

欧阳修

轻舟短棹西湖好，
绿水逶迤。
芳草长堤。
隐隐笙歌处处随。

无风水面琉璃滑，
不觉船移。
微动涟漪。
惊起沙禽掠岸飞。

Gathering Mulberries·
Boat and Oar on West Lake—A Fine Scene

Ouyang Xiu

Boat 'nd oar on West Lake—a fine scene,

The waves wind, green.

Grassy banks long,

Off and on all around me comes a song.

Windless, the surface as smooth as glass shows,

Th' boat rarely goes.

Ripples expand,

Startling water birds to rise from the sand.

采桑子·平生为爱西湖好

欧阳修

平生为爱西湖好，
来拥朱轮。
富贵浮云，
俯仰流年二十春。

归来恰似辽东鹤，
城郭人民。
触目皆新。
谁识当年旧主人。

Gathering Mulberries·
All My Long Life in Love with the West Lake

Ouyang Xiu

All my long life in love of the West Lake,
Gov'rnor I make.
Th' rank's cloud in th' sky;
Before I know, twenty springs have gone by.

Just like the Liaodong Crane I come back in,
Town 'nd folks have been,
New through and through,
Th' then governor, anyone still knows you?

诉衷情

欧阳修

清晨帘幕卷轻霜。
呵手试梅妆。
都缘自有离恨，
故画作远山长。

思往事，
惜流芳。
易成伤。
拟歌先敛，
欲笑还颦，
最断人肠。

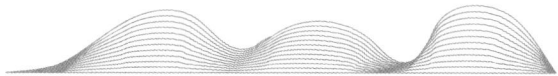

Telling the Innermost Feelings

Ouyang Xiu

At twilight, screen rolled up, light frost I saw,
'Nd blew to hands, th' plum makeup to draw.
All owing to the parting sigh,
I drew mountains over the eye.

Past years to mind,
For them I pined,
Sorrow to bring.
You'd hold the smile to sing,
'Nd smile with a frown to make;
The heart it can best break.

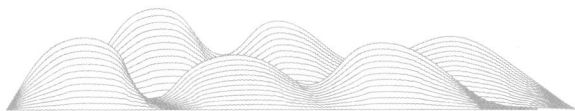

玉楼春

欧阳修

别后不知君远近。

触目凄凉多少闷。

渐行渐远渐无书，

水阔鱼沉何处问。

夜深风竹敲秋韵。

万叶千声皆是恨。

故欹单枕梦中寻，

梦又不成灯又烬。

Jade Tower in Spring

Ouyang Xiu

Since we part, I don't know you are far or nigh,

How much boredom to heart, gloom to the eye.

The further you go, th' fewer mails you send;

Where can I ask, messages to descend?

Th' night leads bamboo to th' fall sound as winds blow,

Thousands of leaves-made sounds to parting woe.

On the lone pillow for dreams, I'd find you;

Candles to ash, the dream does not come true.

73

采桑子

欧阳修

群芳过后西湖好，
狼藉残红。
飞絮濛濛。
垂柳阑干尽日风。

笙歌散尽游人去，
始觉春空。
垂下帘栊。
双燕归来细雨中。

Gathering Mulberries

Ouyang Xiu

Gone as flowers are, fine the West Lake lies;
A mess withered reds stay.
The misty catkin flies.
In the wind drooping willows crisscross sway.

Flute and songs down, fun had, off tourists go;
I just feel spring in vain.
I put the curtain low.
Paired swallows return in the drizzly rain.

蝶恋花

欧阳修

庭院深深深几许。
杨柳堆烟，
帘幕无重数。
玉勒雕鞍游冶处。
楼高不见章台路。

雨横风狂三月暮。
门掩黄昏，
无计留春住。
泪眼问花花不语。
乱红飞过秋千去。

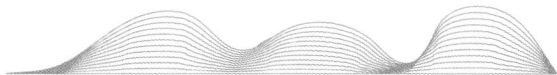

The Butterfly in Love with Blooms

Ouyang Xiu

The courtyard is deep, deep, how very deep!
Heaps 'nd mists of willow flakes,
Screens upon screens of th' heavy heap.
With th' spur, on th' carved saddle, merry he makes.
The tower high, track of him I can't keep.

Spring late, the third moon fierce wind and rain bring.
The gate bars out dusk gloom;
It can do nothing to keep spring.
With tears I ask blooms, no reply's from whom.
A riot of reds fly over the swing.

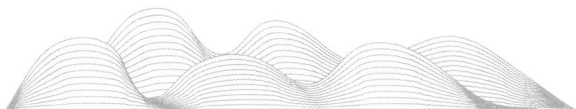

清平乐

王安国

留春不住。
费尽莺儿语。
满地残红宫锦污。
昨夜南园风雨。

小怜初上琵琶。
晓来思绕天涯。
不肯画堂朱户，
春风自在杨花。

The Pure Serene Tune

Wang Anguo

Spring cannot be let stay.
Whatever the orioles say.
Fallen red over th' ground like th' brocade stain,
Last night the south garden was swept by rain.

For th' first time Xiaolian has a lute to play.
Till dawn to th' sky's end her thought winds its way.
To th' red door or painted hall she'd not be;
Like catkins in spring wind she'd be carefree.

卜算子

王 观

水是眼波横，
山是眉峰聚。
欲问行人去那边？
眉眼盈盈处。

才始送春归，
又送君归去。
若到江南赶上春，
千万和春住。

Divination

Wang Guan

Water, in eyes the ripple lies;
Mountains, the ridges of brows rise.
May I ask where the passers-by are bound?
Where clear eyes and brows are around.

I have just sent the spring away;
I then see you on th' homeward way.
If it's spring when to the south you arrive,
In the spring landscape you must live.

蝶恋花

苏 轼

花褪残红青杏小。
燕子飞时，
绿水人家绕。
枝上柳绵吹又少。
天涯何处无芳草。

墙里秋千墙外道。
墙外行人，
墙里佳人笑。
笑渐不闻声渐悄。
多情却被无情恼。

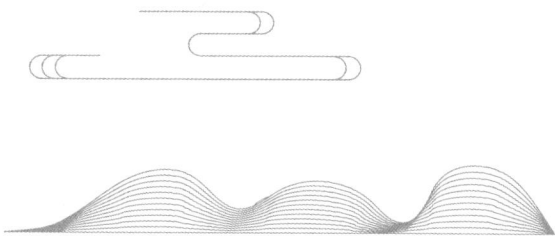

The Butterfly in Love with Flowers

Su Shi

Flowers' colour fades, green apricots small.
When swallows fly their way,
Green water rounds the garden wall.
Willow catkins on twigs blown, fewer stay.
There's not a place where there's no grass at all.

Outside th' wall is a path, inside a swing.
Outside are passers-by,
Inside the belles' laughter does ring.
The laughter unheard, fading by and by.
Th' enchanted th' affectionlessness does sting.

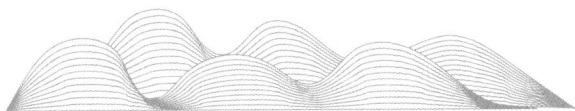

水调歌头

苏 轼

明月几时有，
把酒问青天。
不知天上宫阙，
今夕是何年。
我欲乘风归去，
又恐琼楼玉宇，
高处不胜寒。
起舞弄清影，
何似在人间。

转朱阁，
低绮户，
照无眠。
不应有恨，
何事长向别时圆。
人有悲欢离合，
月有阴晴圆缺，
此事古难全。
但愿人长久，
千里共婵娟。

Prelude to Water Melody

Su Shi

How often does the full moon show?
Wine cup in hand, I ask the sky.
On the celestial palace I don't know,
What year it is today on high.
I intend to ride the wind to go there.
I'm afraid of the towers made of jade;
The cold over there I can't bear.
With the shadow I've danced and played.
How is it like I'm on man's where?

Around the mansions red,
On th' gauze window below,
To th' sleepless th' moonlight's shed.
No spite for man should go.
Why is the moon full when parting remains?
Man, parting and united, has woe 'nd joy;
The moon, shining or hidden, waxes 'nd wanes.
From of old, both rare to enjoy.
As old as we can may we grow!
Miles apart, we'll share th' moonlight flow.

江城子

苏　轼

十年生死两茫茫。
不思量。
自难忘。
千里孤坟，
无处话凄凉。
纵使相逢应不识，
尘满面，
鬓如霜。

夜来幽梦忽还乡。
小轩窗。
正梳妆。
相顾无言，
惟有泪千行。
料得年年断肠处，
明月夜，
短松冈。

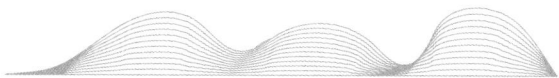

The Riverside Town

Su Shi

For ten years, far are the living 'nd the dead.
To thought it is not led.
It is hard to forget.
Far away th' lone tomb's set.
With no one I can share my gloom.
Even if we meet, she won't know it's whom,
Colour whose face has lost,
Whose temple hair's like frost.

In my dream of last night hometown I see.
At the window was she,
Making up 'nd combing hair.
Mute, at th' other we stare.
Down th' mere lines of tears flow.
Th' place breaks my heart year upon year, I know,
Where th' bright moon at night shines,
On the tomb mound with pines.

念奴娇·赤壁怀古

苏 轼

大江东去，
浪淘尽、
千古风流人物。
故垒西边，
人道是，
三国周郎赤壁。
乱石穿空，
惊涛拍岸，
卷起千堆雪。
江山如画，
一时多少豪杰。

遥想公瑾当年，
小乔初嫁了，
雄姿英发。
羽扇纶巾，
谈笑间、
樯橹灰飞烟灭。
故国神游，
多情应笑我，
早生华发。
人生如梦，
一尊还酹江月。

Charm of a Maiden Singer·In Memory of the Red Cliff

Su Shi

Eastward the River flows;

With the billows that rise,

The hero through the ages goes.

West of th' old fortress lies,

As everybody said,

Red Cliff where Zhou Yu won the war.

To the sky rocks have led,

Like huge waves to the shore,

Roll up a thousand heaps of snow.

Th' land like th' picture to draw,

How many heroes of th' time show.

To mind is Gongjin of those days,

When th' younger Qiao married the man,

Of the heroic rays.

In hand was th' feather fan;

Between laughs, with things planned,

Smoke 'nd ashes foe ships came to be.

My soul roams the old land;

"You gloomy," they would laugh at me;

Early my hair turns grey.

Life's like in th' dream are we,

A toast to the-stream moon I pay.

望江南·超然台作

苏　轼

春未老，
风细柳斜斜。
试上超然台上看，
半壕春水一城花。
烟雨暗千家。

寒食后，
酒醒却咨嗟。
休对故人思故国，
且将新火试新茶。
诗酒趁年华。

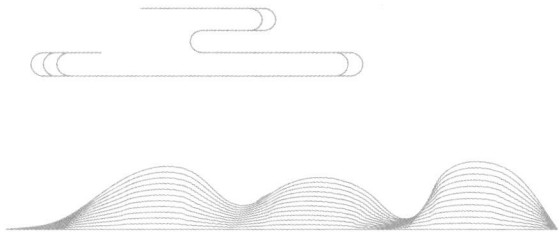

Looking to the South·On the Chaoran Terrace

Su Shi

The spring has not gone by;
The wickers slant as the breeze blows.
On the Chaoran Terrace what comes to th' eye,
The moat half full, with blooms th' town overflows.
All households in gloom th' rain does dye.

After the Cold Food Day,
Awake from th' drunken sleep I sigh.
Of your homesickness to old friends, don't say;
New tea cooked over th' new-made fire, just try.
While young, write poems and have wine, pray.

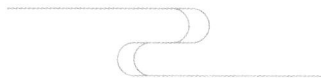

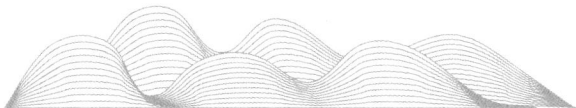

西江月

苏 轼

世事一场大梦，
人生几度秋凉。
夜来风叶已鸣廊。
看取眉头鬓上。

酒贱常愁客少，
月明多被云妨。
中秋谁与共孤光。
把盏凄然北望。

The Moon over the West River

Su Shi

The world is but a dream at all;
In life how many times comes fall?
Th' passage echoes with wind-blown leaves at night
See me on the brows and hair white.

I'm concerned, guests few with wine low;
Clouds oft don't allow th' moon to show.
I'd share th' lone mid-fall moon, whom to be had.
Cup in hand, to look north I'm sad.

定风波

苏 轼

莫听穿林打叶声，
何妨吟啸且徐行。
竹杖芒鞋轻胜马，
谁怕？
一蓑烟雨任平生。

料峭春风吹酒醒，
微冷，
山头斜照却相迎。
回首向来萧瑟处，
归去，
也无风雨也无晴。

Calming Wind and Waves

Su Shi

To th' rain beating leaves through trees don't attend.
Why don't you ease with chant and roar ahead?
Light sandals 'nd cane outdo th' steed to ascend?
Who is in dread?
In cape against the rain, my life I spend.

I'm sobered up as th' spring wind blows its way,
A small bit chill;
To me the sun atop the hill slants th' ray.
I turn around to where soughs 'nd rustles fill;
Back I will go,
With wind, rain or a fine day not to know.

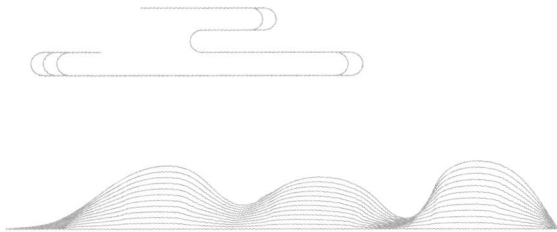

卜算子

苏 轼

缺月挂疏桐，
漏断人初静。
谁见幽人独往来，
缥缈孤鸿影。

惊起却回头，
有恨无人省。
拣尽寒枝不肯栖，
寂寞沙洲冷。

Divination

Su Shi

Th' waning moon over th' phoenix trees,
The hourglass stops and hushed is man.
The recluse comes and goes alone, who sees,
The dim shadow of a lone swan?

With a start, he then turns his head;
He has woe, which none get to know.
All chill twigs checked, to rest he'd not be led.
To the lonely shoal he does go.

浣溪沙

苏 轼

山下兰芽短浸溪。
松间沙路净无泥。
萧萧暮雨子规啼。

谁道人生无再少，
门前流水尚能西。
休将白发唱黄鸡。

Yarn Washing

Su Shi

Orchid buds at th' foot of hill the stream steeps;
Out of mud the sand path through the pines keeps.
In the rustling dusk rain the cuckoo cheeps.

Who says one's unable to gain youth once more?
The stream can flow west in front of the door.
Do not you with grey hair sing time of yore.

临江仙·夜归临皋

苏 轼

夜饮东坡醒复醉，
归来仿佛三更。
家童鼻息已雷鸣。
敲门都不应，
倚杖听江声。

长恨此身非我有，
何时忘却营营。
夜阑风静縠纹平。
小舟从此逝，
江海寄余生。

Celestial Beings by the River· Returning to Lingao at Night

Su Shi

Sober 'nd drunk again at East Slope at night,
I'm back when it's like th' dead of night.
My boy servant gives a thunder of snore;
I knock 'nd he answers not the door.
Against th' cane, I listen to th' river roar.

I'm sad that the body is not my own;
When shall I forget all the drone?
Wind and the river calm, the night does see;
From now on, gone th' small boat will be,
Th' rest of my life on river 'nd sea.

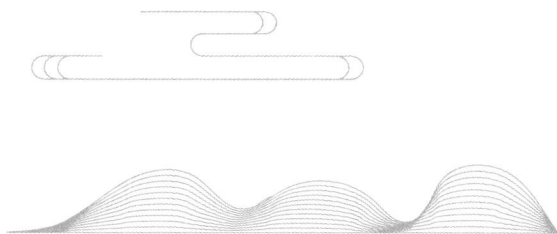

清平乐

晏几道

留人不住。
醉解兰舟去。
一棹碧涛春水路。
过尽晓莺啼处。

渡头杨柳青青。
枝枝叶叶离情。
此后锦书休寄，
画楼云雨无凭。

The Pure Serene Tune

Yan Jidao

I cannot make you stay.
Drunk, you untie th' boat 'nd boat away.
An oar waves up a path of spring.
You pass where the orioles sing.

With willows, the ferry is green,
Of parting woe twigs 'nd leaves have been.
Don't send letters to me from now;
What we shared has no proof of vow.

玉楼春

晏几道

东风又作无情计。
艳粉娇红吹满地。
碧楼帘影不遮愁，
还似去年今日意。

谁知错管春残事。
到处登临曾费泪。
此时金盏直须深，
看尽落花能几醉。

Jade Tower in Spring

Yan Jidao

East wind is being merciless again.
Bright pink and red blown all over th' ground then.
My woe the tower curtain does not shade,
In th' same role of this time of last year played.

God knows to wrong concern th' reduced spring's led;
When I climb heights here and there, tears I shed.
Right now a deep wine cup ought to be got;
All blooms' fall seen, few times I can be th' sot.

生查子

晏几道

关山魂梦长，
鱼雁音尘少。
两鬓可怜青，
只为相思老。

归梦碧纱窗，
说与人人道。
真个别离难，
不似相逢好。

The Green Haw

Yan Jidao

In th' dream th' pass and hills I oft view;
Letters and messages are rare.
It's poor of my black temple hair,
For lovesickness, to have th' old hue.

In th' dream th' green gauze window's in sight;
To th' dearest I open my heart.
It is unbearable to part,
Not as joyous as to unite.

蝶恋花

晏几道

梦入江南烟水路。
行尽江南，
不与离人遇。
睡里消魂无说处。
觉来惆怅消魂误。

欲尽此情书尺素。
浮雁沉鱼，
终了无凭据。
却倚缓弦歌别绪。
断肠移破秦筝柱。

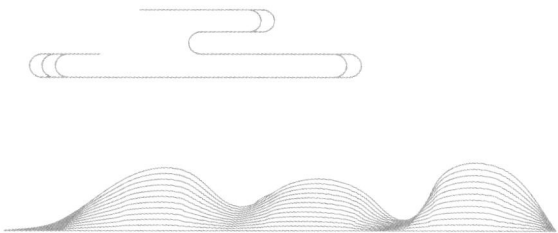

The Butterfly in Love with Blooms

Yan Jidao

In th' dream I roam the misty southern shore.
Across South Land I go,
Not to meet the one I adore.
In the sleep with no one to share my woe,
Awake, I'm seized by woe in th' dream I bore.

The sadness with you through letters to share,
Wild geese soar 'nd fish sink low,
The letters not sent anywhere.
I can but pluck the strings to sing my woe.
String post to break, th' sad heart can't be laid bare.

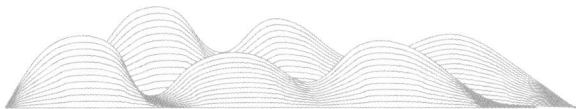

鹧鸪天

黄庭坚

黄菊枝头生晓寒。
人生莫放酒杯干。
风前横笛斜吹雨，
醉里簪花倒著冠。

身健在，
且加餐。
舞裙歌板尽清欢。
黄花白发相牵挽，
付与时人冷眼看。

The Partridge in the Sky

Huang Tingjian

Morn chill for gold chrysanthemums to gain,
In your life don't let your dry cup to spare.
Play your flute in the wind and slanting rain,
Drunk, the hat upside down and blooms to wear.

Should health there be,
Dine and drink more.
With dances and songs, we go on a spree.
The golden flowers for white hair to draw,
I let others glance a cold glance at me.

卜算子

李之仪

我住长江头，
君住长江尾。
日日思君不见君，
共饮长江水。

此水何时休，
此恨何日已。
只愿君心似我心，
定不负相思意。

Divination

Li Zhiyi

I live upstream of the river;
You live downstream of the river.
Day by day I miss you but don't see you;
Drinking from th' river, we both do.

When will the water no more flow?
When will my woe no longer grow?
If only your heart were like mine,
I must live up to heart of thine.

忆秦娥·用太白韵

李之仪

清溪咽。
霜风洗出山头月。
山头月。
迎得云归，
还送云别。

不知今是何时节。
凌歊望断音尘绝。
音尘绝。
帆来帆去，
天际双阙。

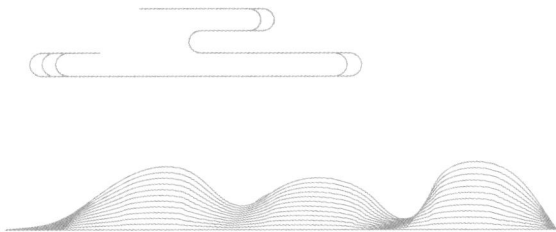

Qin E to Mind·Using Li Bai's Rhyme

Li Zhiyi

Th' clear stream does croon;
The frost and wind wash out the hilltop moon.
The hilltop moon,
Welcomes the clouds on high,
And sees them off with bye.

What season it is today I don't know;
On the heights I see no trace of you show.
Trace not to show,
The sail does come and leave;
In sight two towers heave.

鹊桥仙

秦 观

纤云弄巧，
飞星传恨，
银汉迢迢暗度。
金风玉露一相逢，
便胜却人间无数。

柔情似水，
佳期如梦，
忍顾鹊桥归路。
两情若是久长时，
又岂在朝朝暮暮。

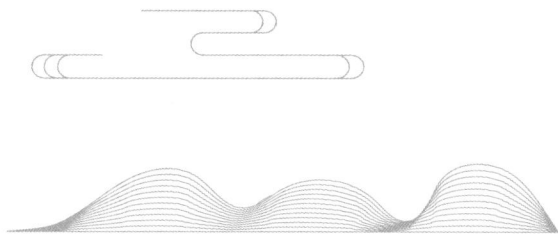

Celestial Beings over Magpie Bridge

Qin Guan

Changes made in clouds light,
Woe carried in stars bright,
Th' Milky Way Cowherd and the Maid steal through;
On meeting of autumn wind 'nd White Dew th' two;
Numerous earthly mortals they outdo.

Like soft water love flows;
Like a dream good time goes;
One's afraid to look back at th' Milky Way.
If they are in love, and in love they stay,
Why must they be together night and day?

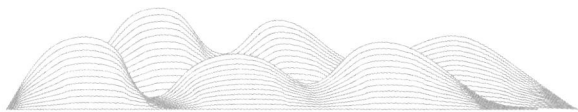

好事近·梦中作

秦 观

春路雨添花，
花动一山春色。
行到小溪深处，
有黄鹂千百。

飞云当面化龙蛇，
夭矫转空碧。
醉卧古藤阴下，
了不知南北。

Good Event Drawing Near·In a Dream

Qin Guan

On spring trails the rain let out blooms;
Blooms stir and the spring scene of the hill booms.
I come to the far end where the stream goes;
The oriole in thousand shows.

Before you, into dragons 'nd snakes clouds fly,
Curling and stretching in the sky.
In the shade of the old vines lies a sot;
It's South or North, I can tell not.

虞美人

秦 观

高城望断尘如雾，
不见联骖处。
夕阳村外小湾头，
只有柳花无数、送归舟。

琼枝玉树频相见。
只恨离人远。
欲将幽事寄青楼，
争奈无情江水、不西流！

Beautiful Lady Yu

Qin Guan

From high walls I see but mistlike dust flies,
The place where we met does not show;
At sunset out the village the bend lies;
Only countless willow catkins see your boat go.

Time to see jade twigs and trees I oft spend;
Far from you I just hate to rest.
Secret woe to your grey mansion I'd send;
However, th' heartless river water flows not west!

画堂春

秦 观

落红铺径水平池。
弄晴小雨霏霏。
杏园憔悴杜鹃啼。
无奈春归。

柳外画楼独上，
凭栏手捻花枝。
放花无语对斜晖。
此恨谁知。

Spring in the Painted Hall

Qin Guan

The pool full, the path strewed with fallen red,
Spitting drizzles have come and fled.
The Apricot Park reduced, cuckoos sing,
No choice to see off spring.

Alone I mount th' willowside to'er;
On th' rail I twiddle a flower.
In th' slanting sun I mutely let it go.
Who knows this very woe?

减字木兰花

秦 观

天涯旧恨。
独自凄凉人不问。
欲见回肠。
断尽金炉小篆香。

黛蛾长敛。
任是春风吹不展。
困倚危楼。
过尽飞鸿字字愁。

The Reduced Magnolia

Qin Guan

Far, old woe to be had,
About my loneliness enquires no one.
You'd want to see I'm sad,
Like the incense in the gold censor done.

Knitted black brows oft lie;
Brows apart, just the east wind cannot blow.
Tired, I lean on th' to'er high;
The passing wild geese fly a flight of woe.

浣溪沙

秦 观

漠漠轻寒上小楼。
晓阴无赖似穷秋。
淡烟流水画屏幽。

自在飞花轻似梦，
无边丝雨细如愁。
宝帘闲挂小银钩。

Yarn Washing

Qin Guan

Up th' tower light prevailing cold does loom.
Rascally like deep autumn is dawn gloom.
On the painted screen lie mist and the stream.

Carefree, the petals fly as light as dream,
Boundless, drizzles fall like my woeful look.
Th' gemmed curtain hangs idly from th' silver hook.

青玉案

贺　铸

凌波不过横塘路。
但目送、芳尘去。
锦瑟华年谁与度。
月桥花院，
琐窗朱户。
只有春知处。

飞云冉冉蘅皋暮。
彩笔新题断肠句。
试问闲愁都几许。
一川烟草，
满城风絮。
梅子黄时雨。

Green Jade Tray

He Zhu

Across the lane her light steps do not cleave.
I watch her rise like dust and leave.
With whom does she have her best time to share?
Th' moon deck, th' yard of blooms fair,
Shut window, and door red.
Only spring knows where to be led.

Dusk falls on th' grassy shore, clouds in slow flight.
Heart-breaking lines of art I newly write.
If you ask me how much my woe would be,
Th' misty grass plain you'd see,
Catkins all over town,
Or rain that falls until plums brown.

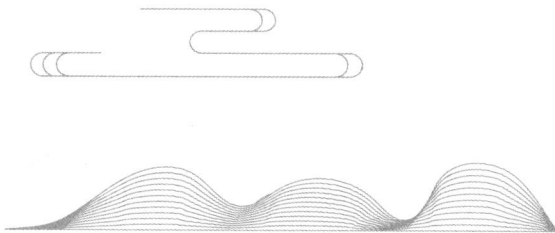

清平乐

贺 铸

厌厌别酒。

更执纤纤手。

指似归期庭下柳。

一叶西风前后。

无端不系孤舟。

载将多少离愁。

又是十分明月，

照人两处登楼。

The Pure Serene Tune

He Zhu

Content with farewell wine,

I held your hands slender and fine.

Return date refers to th' yard willow trees;

Around first leaf fall in west breeze.

Somehow I'm in th' untethered boat,

How much parting woe's held afloat?

The moon again shines fully bright;

We climb two towers it does light.

浣溪沙

贺 铸

不信芳春厌老人。
老人几度送余春。
惜春行乐莫辞频。

巧笑艳歌皆我意，
恼花颠酒拼君瞋。
物情惟有醉中真。

Yarn Washing

He Zhu

I don't think the sweet spring hates the old man.
How many springs in his life will he scan?
Spring to cherish, pleasure I don't oft ban.

For fine smiles and romantic songs I'm glad;
Despite your glare, for blooms and wine I'm mad,
When I'm drunk, the true feelings to be had.

忆少年·别历下

晁补之

无情官柳，
无情画舸，
无根行客。
南山尚相送，
只高城人隔。

罨画园林溪绀碧，
算重来、尽成陈迹。
刘郎鬓如此，
况桃花颜色。

A Recollection of Youth·Farewell at Lixia

Chao Buzhi

Willows to have no bound,
Heartless fun boats to stay,
Travellers to go round,
Mt. South still sees me go away;
Just sight's barred of belles on high ground.

Like colour-painting are parks, streams clear 'nd green;
They'd be things of yore if I came anew.
Such Mr. Liu's temple hair has been,
Let alone the peach blossom's hue.

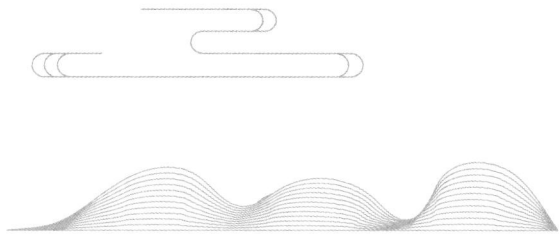

临江仙

晁冲之

忆昔西池池上饮，
年年多少欢娱。
别来不寄一行书。
寻常相见了，
犹道不如初。

安稳锦衾今夜梦，
月明好渡江湖。
相思休问定何如。
情知春去后，
管得落花无。

Celestial Beings by the River

Chao Chongzhi

The feast on the West Pool to mind of yore,
How much year-to-year joy we've had!
Since he leaves, he's not sent word any more.
Even if I do meet the lad,
It's said to be unlike before.

For tonight's dream the silken quilt laid there,
With th' moonlight I'd cross rivers 'nd lakes.
Him as I miss, I don't ask how things fare.
Up to the end of spring one wakes;
Whether blooms have fallen, who'll care.

少年游·并刀如水

周邦彦

并刀如水，
吴盐胜雪，
纤手破新橙。
锦幄初温，
兽烟不断，
相对坐调笙。

低声问向谁行宿，
城上已三更。
马滑霜浓，
不如休去，
直是少人行。

Youth's Travels·Sharp Knives Bingzhou Did Yield

Zhou Bangyan

Sharp knives Bingzhou did yield;
Wu's salt has th' snow-white hue;
The new oranges slim hands peeled.
In th' bed screen warmth just grew;
Out the Beast, the smoke speeled;
Just across the flute sit the two.

A low voice says, where tonight are you bound?
The night's already deepened so;
The horse'd slip on th' frost ground;
You had better not go;
In the street few strollers are found.

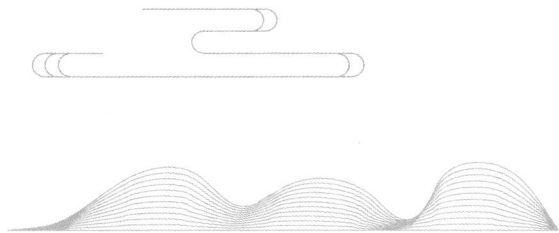

惜分飞

毛　滂

泪湿阑干花著露。

愁到眉峰碧聚。

此恨平分取。

更无言语。空相觑。

断雨残云无意绪。

寂寞朝朝暮暮。

今夜山深处。

断魂分付。潮回去。

Separation to Feel Sorry for

Mao Pang

Tears over the face, like dew that blooms wear,

My eyebrows knitted, woe has made.

The woe we do equally share.

We say nothing, eyes on each other laid.

No mood the broken rain and cloud bring me.

I'm lonely all night and all day.

Tonight, in deep mountains I'll be.

My soul'll bid the tide go on th' return way.

蝶恋花

赵令畤

欲减罗衣寒未去。
不卷珠帘，
人在深深处。
红杏枝头花几许。
啼痕止恨清明雨。

尽日沉烟香一缕。
宿酒醒迟，
恼破春情绪。
飞燕又将归信误。
小屏风上西江路。

The Butterfly in Love with Blooms

Zhao Lingzhi

Clothes to reduce, not to go is cold.
The bead curtain unrolled,
I'm deep somewhere, its depth untold.
How many apri'ot blooms on twigs remain?
With tears' trace, I loathe but th' Clear and Bright rain.

All day a breath of incense smoke to take,
From hango'er, late I wake,
So sad about the spring to break.
Sending messages swallows will delay.
On the little screen is the water way.

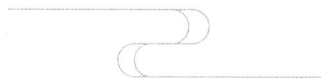

清平乐

赵令畤

春风依旧。
著意隋堤柳。
搓得蛾儿黄欲就。
天气清明时候。

去年紫陌青门。
今宵雨魄云魂。
断送一生憔悴，
只销几个黄昏。

The Pure Serene Tune

Zhao Lingzhi

The spring wind as before
Loves willows grown on th' bank of yore,
Kneading them to gosling-yellow on th' tree.
Th' weather's how Clear and Bright would be.

Last year's blue gate 'nd capital lane,
Tonight's psyche of cloud 'nd soul of rain.
A pining and ruined life to lead,
Only a few such dusks to need.

虞美人

叶梦得

落花已作风前舞。
又送黄昏雨。
晓来庭院半残红。
惟有游丝千丈、
胃晴空。

殷勤花下同携手。
更尽杯中酒。
美人不用敛蛾眉。
我亦多情、
无奈酒阑时。

Beautiful Lady Yu

Ye Mengde

In the wind the fallen blooms in dance fly.
Again the dusk rain's seen to go.
Withered reds on half the yard, dawn comes by.
Just a thousand-foot wisp to show
Curls in th' clear sky.

Neath blooms, hand in hand, together we sit.
Let me drink the cupped wine with you.
My belle, do you not have your eyebrows knit.
I am in sorrow too;
When wine's drunk up, I can't help it.

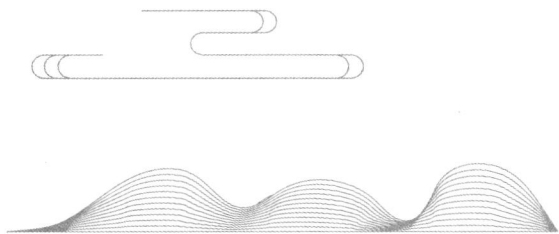

清平乐

刘一止

相望吴楚。

远信无凭据。

欲倩春风吹泪去。

化作愁云恨雨。

春应已到三吴。

楚江日夜东徂。

惟有溯流鱼上,

不知尺素来无。

The Pure Serene Tune

Liu Yizhi

At Wu and Chu are we,

Far apart, no letters to me.

I'd ask spring wind to blow my tears to go,

Transformed into clouds 'nd rain of woe.

In three Wus spring must have begun.

Day and night th' Chu River does run.

Only fish that up the stream go,

Whether letters come, they don't know.

菩萨蛮

陈 克

赤阑桥尽香街直。

笼街细柳娇无力。

金碧上青空。

花晴帘影红。

黄衫飞白马。

日日青楼下。

醉眼不逢人。

午香吹暗尘。

The Buddha Envoy

Chen Ke

The Red Rail Bridge joins the sweet-smelling street,

Willows shading the street, tender and weak.

Splendid towers up to the sky,

Sun-lit blooms through screens, red to th' eye.

Golden clothes on the steed fly,

Out th' brothel each day, th' steed to tie,

None is present in his drunk eyes,

Amid sweet scent, dirt stirred to rise.

菩萨蛮

陈 克

绿芜墙绕青苔院。
中庭日淡芭蕉卷。
蝴蝶上阶飞。
烘帘自在垂。

玉钩双语燕。
宝甃杨花转。
几处簸钱声。
绿窗春睡轻。

The Buddha Envoy

Chen Ke

Walls overgrown with grass round th' moss-strewn yard,
Banana leaves roll, th' sun to th' atrium barred.
Butterflies over the steps soar.
At ease droops the curtain of door.

Above the hooks two swallows cry.
Round th' well wall willow catkins fly.
In a few places coins to fling,
Inside th' screen one sleeps away spring.

豆叶黄

陈 克

秋千人散小庭空。
麝冷灯昏愁杀侬。
独有闲阶两袖风。
月胧胧。
一树梨花细雨中。

Bean Leaves Brown

Chen Ke

The courtyard left empty, the swing all leave.
My woe the incense cold 'nd the dim lamp weave.
I'm alone on the steps, wind in each sleeve.
The moon in gloom,
In fine rain is a tree of the pear bloom.

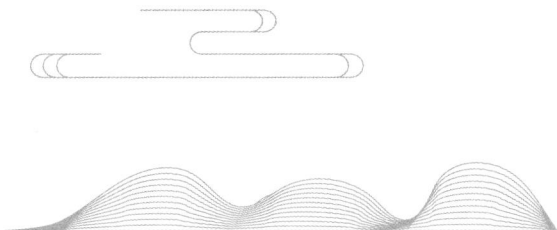

一落索

朱敦儒

一夜雨声连晓，
青灯相照。
旧时情绪此时心，
花不见、
人空老。

可惜春光闲了，
阴多晴少。
江南江北水连天，
问何处、
寻芳草？

A String of Entwined Words

Zhu Dunru

From night to dawn patters the rain;
The lamp light glows on me.
The woe of the past now comes on the brain;
Blooms not to see,
I'm old in vain.

It's a shame that spring idles by,
Gloom common, brightness rare.
Water north and south of th' river joins th' sky.
I would ask where
For grass you try?

南歌子

李　祁

袅袅秋风起，
萧萧败叶声。
岳阳楼上听哀筝。
楼下凄凉江月、
为谁明。

雾雨沉云梦，
烟波渺洞庭。
可怜无处问湘灵。
只有无情江水、
绕孤城。

The Southern Song

Li Qi

Rises a wreath of autumn breeze;
Withered leaves rustle down from trees.
On Yueyang To'er, sad zither tunes I hear;
The moon over the river drear
Rays for which dear?

To Cloud 'nd Dream Swamps mist 'nd rain are fed;
Over Dongting Lake mist 'nd waves spread.
A shame: to the river god I'm not led,
Just the heartless river flows down
Round th' river town.

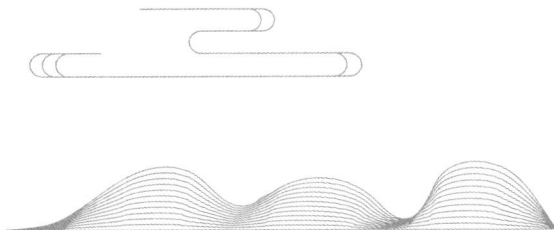

添字采桑子

李清照

窗前谁种芭蕉树？
阴满中庭。
阴满中庭，
叶叶心心，
舒卷有馀情。

伤心枕上三更雨，
点滴霖霪。
点滴霖霪，
愁损北人，
不惯起来听。

The Increased Gathering Mulberries

Li Qingzhao

Who has built the plantain by the window,
Casting a court shadow?
Casting a court shadow,
Leaves rolls and unrolls my sorrow.

Sad, head on pillow mid a mid-night rain,
Pattering on the pane,
Pattering on the pane,
My poor self in such pain
Won't listen to th' patters, in vain.

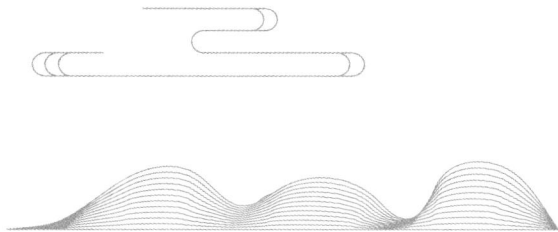

如梦令·常记溪亭日暮

李清照

常记溪亭日暮。

沉醉不知归路。

兴尽晚回舟，

误入藕花深处。

争渡。争渡。

惊起一滩鸥鹭。

Like a Dream·Stream, Arbor and Dusk Oft Come to My Mind

Li Qingzhao

Stream, arbor and dusk oft come to my mind,

I'm drunk, th' thought of going home thrown behind.

Fun had till late, I took to th' boat;

Deep into th' lotuses I strayed afloat.

To pole th' boat through, to pole th' boat through,

I startled the egrets and up they flew.

如梦令·昨夜雨疏风骤

李清照

昨夜雨疏风骤。

浓睡不消残酒。

试问卷帘人，

却道海棠依旧。

知否。知否。

应是绿肥红瘦。

Like a Dream·Last Night the Wind Rages
with Little Rain

Li Qingzhao

Last night the wind rages with little rain;

Sound sleep does not dispel wine in the vein.

To ask th' curtain folder I try;

"The begonia looks the same" is th' reply.

Do you not know, do you not now?

The red should be gone and the green should grow.

武陵春

李清照

风住尘香花已尽，
日晚倦梳头。
物是人非事事休，
欲语泪先流。

闻说双溪春尚好，
也拟泛轻舟。
只恐双溪舴艋舟，
载不动许多愁。

Spring at Wuling

Li Qingzhao

Wind comes to an end, with dirt sweet, blooms fall;
I'd not comb hair, though up th' sun goes.
Things th' same, with him no more, over is all.
Ere I'm to speak, the tear first flows.

As is said, at Twin Creek spring has still stayed;
Rowing a boat I plan to go.
At the Twin Creek the boat, I am afraid,
Is unable to hold much of my woe.

一剪梅

李清照

红藕香残玉簟秋。
轻解罗裳，
独上兰舟。
云中谁寄锦书来？
雁字回时，
月满西楼。

花自飘零水自流。
一种相思，
两处闲愁。
此情无计可消除，
才下眉头，
却上心头。

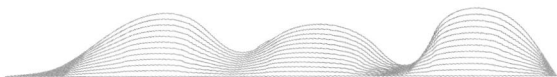

A Spray of Plum Blossoms

Li Qingzhao

Th' sweet lotus gone, fall the jade-like mat's shown;
Off my silk robe to be,
I board the boat alone.
Who in the cloud would bring letters to me?
Wild geese on their back flight,
My tower th' moon does light.

Flowers drift and water itself does flow;
Lovesickness of a kind,
From two places is woe.
There's no way to remove this love from mind,
Eyebrows to just descend,
My heart to but ascend.

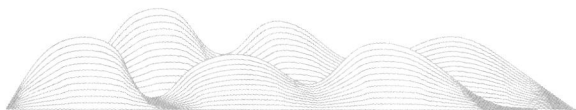

醉花阴

李清照

薄雾浓云愁永昼。
瑞脑消金兽。
佳节又重阳，
玉枕纱厨，
半夜凉初透。

东篱把酒黄昏后。
有暗香盈袖。
莫道不销魂，
帘卷西风，
人比黄花瘦。

Tipsy in the Flower Shade

Li Qingzhao

Mist thin and cloud thick, I'm sad all long day;
Incense in Gold Beast burns away.
Again comes the Double Ninth Day;
Th' silk screen 'nd pillow of jade
The midnight chill first does invade.

At dusk I had wine before the east fence,
My sleeves with subtle fragrance thence.
Don't say I'm not deprived of sense,
Th' curtain raised by west wind.
Than the yellow blooms I've more thinned.

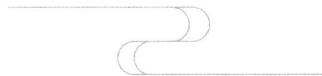

点绛唇

李清照

寂寞深闺，
柔肠一寸愁千缕。
惜春春去。
几点催花雨。

倚遍阑干，
只是无情绪。
人何处。
连天芳草，
望断归来路。

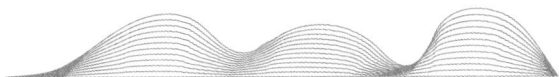

The Touch of the Rouged Lip

Li Qingzhao

Loneliness my room sows;
An inch of love's a thousand threads of gloom;
Cherished though, the spring goes,
A few raindrops hasten the bloom.

From rail to rail I lean;
Only that my spirits are none.
Where has he been?
To th' sky green grass does run;
His way back is seen till unseen.

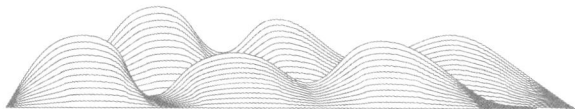

采桑子

吕本中

恨君不似江楼月，
南北东西。
南北东西。
只有相随无别离。

恨君却似江楼月，
暂满还亏。
暂满还亏。
待得团圆是几时。

Gathering Mulberries

Lv Benzhong

I'm sad: like th' ri'er tower moon you won't be,
North, south, east 'nd west.
North, south, east 'nd west,
In company, the moon won't part with me.

But like th' ri'ver tower moon you'll be, I'm sad;
It waxes 'nd wanes.
It waxes 'nd wanes,
When's the time for the round moon to be had?

减字木兰花

吕本中

去年今夜，
同醉月明花树下。
此夜江边。
月暗长堤柳暗船。

故人何处。
带我离愁江外去。
来岁花前。
又是今年忆去年。

The Reduced Magnolia

Lv Benzhong

Last year this very night,

The moon bright, we are drunk beneath the blooms.

By the river tonight,

Long banks dimmed by th' moon, th' boat the willow glooms.

Where is my old friend dear?

Beyond the river take my woe to part.

Before the blooms next year,

Like this year I'll bring the past years to heart.

生查子

向子諲

近似月当怀，
远似花藏雾。
好花月明时，
同醉花深处。

看花不自持，
对月空相顾。
愿学月频圆，
莫作花飞去。

The Green Haw

Xiang Ziyin

Near, she's like the moon to my breast to draw;
Far, she's like the bloom in the mist to store.
When the bloom at its best the bright moon's met,
Both drunk in the depth of the blooms let's get.

From watching the blooms I cannot refrain;
With th' moon, we look at each other in vain.
Like the moon that oft goes round, we'd unite;
Don't be the blooms that go away in flight.

卜算子

蔡 伸

前度月圆时，
月下相携手。
今夜天边月又圆，
夜色如清昼。

风月浑依旧。
水馆空回首。
明夜归来试问伊，
曾解思量否。

Divination

Cai Shen

When the moon appears round last night,
Under the moon, hands-joined we stay.
In th' far sky the moon's round again tonight;
The night's like the bright and clear day.

Wind 'nd Moon all the same as they were,
Th' water tower brought to vain mind,
When she comes back I'll attempt to ask her,
How I miss her, if she does find.

长相思

王 灼

来匆匆。
去匆匆。
短梦无凭春又空。
难随郎马踪。

山重重。
水重重。
飞絮流云西复东。
音书何处通。

Long Longing

Wang Zhuo

You come in haste;
You go in haste;
Short dream unevidenced, spring's unreal too;
It is hard to trace your steed's clue.

Hills upon hills,
Rills upon rills,
East 'nd west flying catkins 'nd wafting clouds wend;
Letters to you, where can I send?

151

卜算子

如　晦

有意送春归，
无计留春住。
毕竟年年用著来，
何似休归去。

目断楚天遥，
不见春归路。
风急桃花也似愁，
点点飞红雨。

Divination

Ru Hui

I have th' intent to see spring go;
I have no means to make it stay.
After all, from year to year it would show;
In this case, do not go away!

The Southern Chu's sky my eyes reach;
I can't see the back way spring's led.
In the fierce wind, in woe seem blooms of peach;
Drops upon drops fly, showers red.

忆王孙·春词

李重元

萋萋芳草忆王孙。
柳外高楼空断魂。
杜宇声声不忍闻。
欲黄昏。
雨打梨花深闭门。

A Recollection of My Friend·The Lyric of Spring

Li Chongyuan

Grass lush, I recall th' friend roving somewhere;
My heart breaks, th' by-willow to'er to ascend.
Cuckoos upon cuckoos I cannot bear.
Dusk to descend,
Gate shut, the rain beats blossoms on the pear.

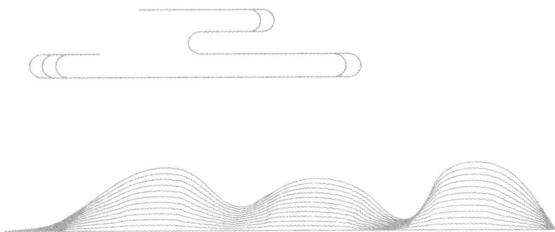

惜分飞·送别

吴淑姬

岸柳依依拖金缕。

是我朝来别处。

惟有多情絮。

故来衣上留人住。

两眼啼红空弹与。

未见桃花又去。

一片征帆举。

断肠遥指苕溪路。

Separation to Feel Sorry for·To Farewell

Wu Shuji

The bank willows gently trail their gold rays,

Where morrow morning I see him depart.

Only the catkin of fond heart,

Thereby onto clothes of his it stays.

I cry my eyes red, strings to vainly play,

Not to see peach blooms go again.

A sail filled to rise on campaign,

I sadly point far to the Tiao Stream Way.

菩萨蛮

李弥逊

江城烽火连三月。
不堪对酒长亭别。
休作断肠声。
老来无泪倾。

风高帆影疾。
目送舟痕碧。
锦字几时来。
薰风无雁回。

The Buddha Envoy

Li Mixun

For three moons beacons in th' river town flare.
Farewell at th' arbour with wine I can't bear.
Your heart-breaking cry you do hold.
I can shed not a tear while old.

Your sail speeds forward as winds rise,
Your sailer's trails green to my eyes.
When will your letters come to me?
Winds warm, back no wild geese would be.

虞美人

陈与义

十年花底承朝露。
看到江南树。
洛阳城里又东风。
未必桃花得似、
旧时红。

胭脂睡起春才好。
应恨人空老。
心情虽在只吟诗。
白髮刘郎孤负、
可怜枝。

Beautiful Lady Yu

Chen Yuyi

For ten years, morning dew for blooms to store,
In th' River South I see th' peach tree.
In Luoyang easterly wind blows once more.
The peach blooms are not sure to be
Red as of yore.

The rouged one wakes up when spring is just best.
I'm vainly old, my sadness true.
I chant poems with the then mind still possessed.
But grey-haired Mr. Liu lives up to
The twigs so blessed.

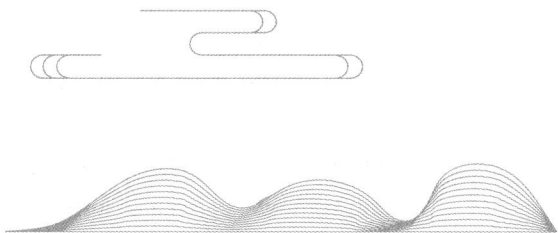

菩萨蛮

张元幹

春来春去催人老。
老大争肯输年少。
醉后少年狂。
白髭殊未妨。

插花还起舞。
管领风光处。
把酒共留春。
莫教花笑人。

The Buddha Envoy

Zhang Yuangan

Spring comes, goes, 'nd prompts me to be an old one;
Aged though, how can I lose to the young son.
Drunk, I'm as proud as the young are.
White beard is really not a bar.

I dance, flowers pinned in the hair,
A master of scenes anywhere.
Wine in hand, let's retain spring here;
Don't let flowers give man a sneer.

卜算子

张元幹

风露湿行云，
沙水迷归艇。
卧看明河月满空，
斗挂苍山顶。

万古只青天，
多事悲人境。
起舞闻鸡酒未解，
潮落秋江冷。

Divination

Zhang Yuangan

With wind 'nd dew, I'm wet when clouds float;
Th' Sand Stream mist gets lost th' return boat.
Lying there, I see th' moon 'nd Milky Way sky;
Over th' hilltop the Plough hangs high.

Forever remains the sky blue;
Many miseries man goes through.
I practise sword at th' rooster's crow, drunk still.
Tides fall, the Autumn River chill.

长相思令

邓 肃

红花飞。
白花飞。
郎与春风同别离。
春归郎不归。

雨霏霏。
雪霏霏。
又是黄昏独掩扉。
孤灯隔翠帷。

Long Longing

Deng Su

Red flowers fly.
White flowers fly.
Together with the spring wind, departs he.
Spring is back but he would not be.

The rain falls hard.
The snow falls hard.
Again, dusk sees the gate closed, I alone.
Out the curtain is the lamp lone.

菩萨蛮

谢明远

春风春雨花经眼。
石泉槐火春容晚。
流水自无情。
回波聚落英。

问春何处去。
春向天边住。
举酒欲销愁。
酒阑愁更愁。

The Buddha Envoy

Xie Mingyuan

To the eyes blooms in spring wind and rain blow.
Spring through stones, spring late, the by-tree fire fumes.
The water flows its heartless flow.
Back ripples gather fallen blooms.

If you ask where spring is to go,
To the end of the sky spring goes.
To life wine is to lift my woe.
With wine finished, woe even grows.

恨欢迟

张 焘

淡薄情怀。
浅缀胭脂。
独占江梅。
最好是、
严凝苦寒天气，
却是开时。

也不许、
桃杏斗妍娤。
也不许、
雪霜相欺。
又只恐、
谁家一声羌笛，
落尽南枝。

Sorry for the Late Joy

Zhang Tao

Indifference to bear,
A little rouge to wear,
On th' wintersweet to rest.
What is the best
Is the weather of bitter cold,
When the blossoms unfold.

It would not let
Peach and apricot vie and met.
It would not let
Snow and frost be the threat.
It's just afraid:
From some home the flute tune is played,
All plum blossoms to raid.

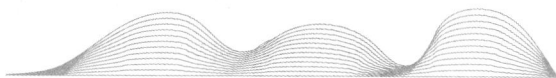

长相思·游西湖

康与之

南高峰。
北高峰。
一月湖光烟霭中。
春来愁杀侬。

郎意浓。
妾意浓。
油壁车轻郎马骢。
相逢九里松。

Long Longing·A Tour of West Lake

Kang Yuzhi

On the south peak,
On the north peak,
I have the lake veiled by the mist to see;
As the spring comes, sorrow kills me.

Your love is deep.
My love is deep.
My painted carriage light, and your steed fine.
We meet along nine miles of th' pine.

南柯子

王　炎

山冥云阴重，
天寒雨意浓。
数枝幽艳湿啼红。
莫为惜花惆怅、
对东风。

蓑笠朝朝出，
沟塍处处通。
人间辛苦是三农。
要得一犁水足、
望年丰。

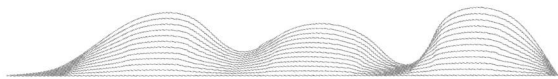

The Fond Dream

Wang Yan

Mountains dark, cloud in heavy gloom,
The weather cold, rain to be had.
A few trees cry wet with dew in th' red bloom.
Pitying the blooms, don't be sad;
At the east wind I fume.

From day to day out straw cloaks go,
On paths between fields here and there.
The hardest are those three seasons to sow;
Who plough fields, no water to spare,
A bumper year to owe.

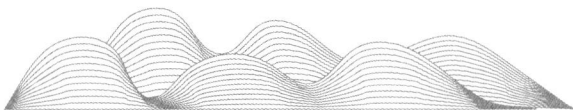

生查子

赵彦端

新月曲如眉，
未有团圆意。
红豆不堪看，
满眼相思泪。

终日擘桃穰，
人在心儿里。
两朵隔墙花，
早晚成连理。

The Green Haw

Zhao Yanduan

Th' new moon's curvous as th' eyebrow's been;
It does not mean to be round yet.
I can't bear to see the red bean;
With lovesick tears my eyes are wet.

All day I break th' peach's core part;
The one I love is in my heart.
Two flowers severed by the wall
Will join to a knot after all.

好事近·登梅仙山绝顶望海

陆　游

挥袖上西峰，
孤绝去天无尺。
挂杖下临鲸海，
数烟帆历历。

贪看云气舞青鸾，
归路已将夕。
多谢半山松吹，
解殷勤留客。

Good Event Drawing Near·
Viewing the Sea on the Wintersweet Celestial Mountain

Lu You

Waving sleeves, I climb th' Peak of West;
Close to th' sky is where th' top does rest.
Cane in hand, I reach th' sea of whales,
Counting mist-veiled sails upon sails.

I'm greedy to see clouds dance in th' blue sky;
It's dusk when on th' way home am I.
It's winds through halfway pines that blow
And that detain the guest I know.

长相思

陆 游

面苍然。
鬓皤然。
满腹诗书不值钱。
官闲常昼眠。

画凌烟。
上甘泉。
自古功名属少年。
知心惟杜鹃。

Long Longing

Lu You

My face is white;
My hair is white.
Having a mind of letters, I'm but cheap.
I idle along through day sleep.

Praised by the king,
Met by the king,
The young are whom glory and names go to.
He who knows me is the cuckoo.

南柯子

范成大

怅望梅花驿，
凝情杜若洲。
香云低处有高楼。
可惜高楼、
不近木兰舟。

缄素双鱼远，
题红片叶秋。
欲凭江水寄离愁。
江水东流、
那肯更西流。

The Fond Dream

Fan Chengda

To the courier station I gaze;
Its love on th' Herb Isle the eye lays.
Where clouds float low, the tower rises high;
Over th' tower I sigh;
To the orchid boat it's not nigh.

It's too far to send word of mine,
With a red leaf to write the line.
I'm to use th' stream to send my parting woe;
East the river does flow;
Westward, how can it mean to go?

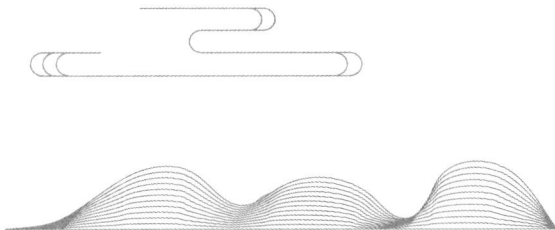

好事近·七月十三日夜
登万花川谷望月作

杨万里

月未到诚斋，
先到万花川谷。
不是诚斋无月，
隔一林修竹。

如今才是十三夜，
月色已如玉。
未是秋光奇绝，
看十五十六。

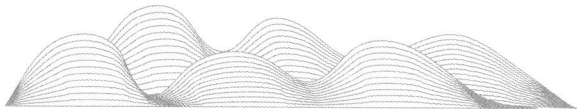

Good Event Drawing Near·
Viewing the Moon at the Vale of Blooms on the
Thirteenth Night of the Seventh Moon

Yang Wanli

In my study no moonlight looms;
It flows first in the Vale of Blooms.
Not that my study sees no moon,
Between is a grove of bamboos.

It is only the thirteenth night tonight;
The moon is already jade-white.
It's not the best of autumn yet;
See the fifteenth and sixteenth's sight.

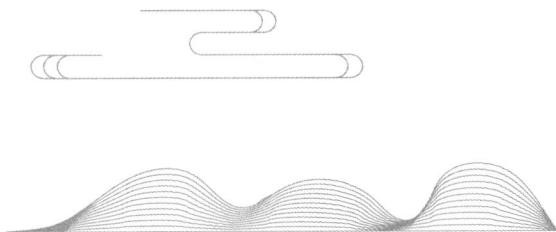

卜算子

严 蕊

不是爱风尘，
似被前缘误。
花落花开自有时，
总赖东君主。

去也终须去，
住也如何住？
若得山花插满头，
莫问奴归处。

Divination

Yan Rui

I love no debauched life to lead,
Which Prelife Fate seems to misread.
There's time for flowers to blow or to fall;
It's up to Lord East after all.

To leave, in th' end I'll go away;
To stay, where and how can I stay?
If I can get wild blooms to strew my head,
Don't ask me where my home is led.

如梦令

严 蕊

道是梨花不是，
道是杏花不是。
白白与红红，
别是东风情味。
曾记，曾记，
人在武陵微醉。

Like a Dream

Yan Rui

Said to be the pear bloom or not?
Said to be th' apricot or not?
White and red, red and white,
East wind brings a unique delight.
Don't forget, don't forget;
Drunk with it th' Wuling man does get.

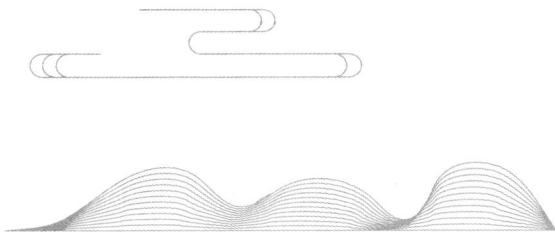

浣溪沙

张孝祥

霜日明霄水蘸空，
鸣鞘声里绣旗红。
淡烟衰草有无中。

万里中原烽火北，
一尊浊酒戍楼东。
酒阑挥泪向悲风。

Yarn Washing

Zhang Xiaoxiang

In th' autumn sun, water joins the clear sky;
With the whippings, red embroidered flags fly.
Light smoke from withered grass faint to the eye.

Miles of Central Plains north of beacon line,
On th' east gate to'er I have a cup of wine,
Wine had, throwing in cold wind tears of mine.

谒金门·春雪

韩元吉

春尚浅。
谁把玉英裁剪。
尽道梅梢开未遍。
卷帘花满院。

楼上酒融歌暖。
楼下水平烟远。
却似涌金门外见。
絮飞波影乱。

Calling at the Golden Gate·Spring Snow

Han Yuanji

Spring's just to show.
The blooms have been tailored by whom?
As said, plum blooms at th' twig's tip yet to blow,
Curtain rolled, all yard with the bloom.

Upstairs warm wine and songs there've been,
Downstairs water calm and mist far.
It's what's outside Yongjin gate to be seen.
Flakes fly, 'nd wild their reflections are.

清平乐·夏日游湖

朱淑真

恼烟撩露。
留我须臾住。
携手藕花湖上路，
一霎黄梅细雨。

娇痴不怕人猜。
和衣睡倒人怀。
最是分携时候，
归来懒傍妆台。

The Pure Serene Tune·
A Tour of the Lake on a Summer Day

Zhu Shuzhen

Vexing mist 'nd teasing dew,
What keeps me awhile is the view.
It's Lotus Lake that hands joined, we roam by.
Plum drizzles fall in the blink of an eye.

Naive, for others' comments I care not;
Undoffed, asleep in his arms I have got.
It's the hardest time that to part is due;
Idle when back, my dresser I'm close to.

谒金门·春半

朱淑真

春已半，
触目此情无限。
十二阑干闲倚遍，
愁来天不管。

好是风和日暖，
输与莺莺燕燕。
满院落花帘不卷，
断肠芳草远。

Calling at the Golden Gate·Mid-spring

Zhu Shuzhen

Passed half of spring;
Infinite sorrow things my eyes meet bring.
Twenty-four hours against all rails I rest;
Heaven doesn't care, woe in chest.

It's good that th' sun is warm, wind fair,
With which orioles and swallows can compare.
Fallen blooms on th' yard, I'd not roll up th' screen;
My heart breaks when far goes th' grass green.

眼儿媚

朱淑真

迟迟春日弄轻柔。
花径暗香流。
清明过了，
不堪回首，
云锁朱楼。

午窗睡起莺声巧，
何处唤春愁。
绿杨影里，
海棠亭畔，
红杏梢头。

Ogling Eyes

Zhu Shuzhen

With the tender the late spring sun rays play;
On bloom-lined paths flows slight sweet air.
Goes the clear bright Tomb Sweeping Day;
To recall bygones I can't bear;
Shrouding the grand tower, clouds stay.

I wake from th' noon nap, 'nd orioles chirp in glee.
Where do th' chirps bring awake spring woe?
In the willow tree's shade to be;
By Begonia Arbour to go;
At the top of th' apricot tree.

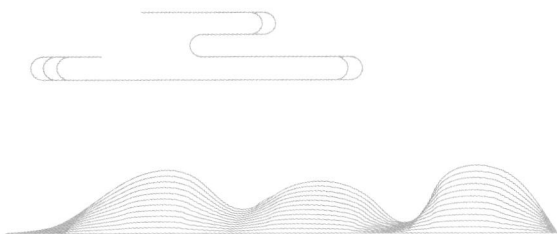

蝶恋花·送春

朱淑真

楼外垂杨千万缕。
欲系青春,
少住春还去。
犹自风前飘柳絮。
随春且看归何处。

绿满山川闻杜宇。
便做无情,
莫也愁人苦。
把酒送青春不语。
黄昏却下潇潇雨。

The Butterfly in Love with Blooms·
Seeing Off Spring

Zhu Shuzhen

Thousands of willows out th' tower astray,
The green spring is to tie,
Which stays a while and gets away.
In the wind willow catkins alone fly,
Following the spring, to what place are they?

Cuckoos heard over hills 'nd rills, green to be;
Heartlessly as they cry,
Are they not feeling sad for me?
Wine in hand, I ask spring who won't reply;
But rustling drizzles fall, at dusk I see.

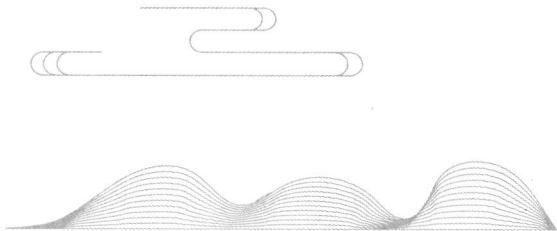

减字木兰花·春怨

朱淑真

独行独坐。
独倡独酬还独卧。
伫立伤神。
无奈轻寒著摸人。

此情谁见。
泪洗残妆无一半。
愁病相仍。
剔尽寒灯梦不成。

The Reduced Magnolia·The Spring Woe

Zhu Shuzhen

I walk and sit alone.
I sing, socialize and sleep on my own.
Standing long, sad I'd be.
I can't help but let the light cold plague me.

Who'd see my pain and woe?
Washing half the makeup off, my tears flow.
Woe and ailment remain.
The wick cut to the end, dreams come in vain.

丑奴儿·书博山道中壁

辛弃疾

少年不识愁滋味，
爱上层楼。
爱上层楼。
为赋新词强说愁。

而今识尽愁滋味，
欲说还休。
欲说还休。
却道天凉好个秋。

The Ugly Slave·Writing on the Wall
on the Way to Mt. Bo

Xin Qiji

Woe the youth does not at all know;

He'd go upstairs.

He'd go upstairs.

For a new verse he forces woe.

Now woe completely he does know;

I'd speak or not.

I'd speak or not.

What cool fall days, he just says so.

破阵子

辛弃疾

醉里挑灯看剑，
梦回吹角连营。
八百里分麾下炙，
五十弦翻塞外声。
沙场秋点兵。

马作的卢飞快，
弓如霹雳弦惊。
了却君王天下事，
赢得生前身后名。
可怜白发生。

The Parade

Xin Qiji

Drunk, stirring th' wick, I checked my sword;
I dreamed of the camp where horns soared.
Th' soldiers share beef to grill I bade;
On the strings *Song of the Frontier* I played.
In fall th' battlefield see th' parade.

Th' steeds like Dilu steeds on the wing,
The bow with a whoosh startled th' string.
I'd complete the king's mission, North to claim,
To win the in-life and after-death name.
My hair turned grey, which is a shame.

西江月·夜行黄沙道中

辛弃疾

明月别枝惊鹊，
清风半夜鸣蝉。
稻花香里说丰年。
听取蛙声一片。

七八个星天外，
两三点雨山前。
旧时茅店社林边。
路转溪桥忽见。

The Moon over the West River·
A Night Trip on the Sand Road

Xin Qiji

Magpies scared off twigs by th' moon bright,
Breeze makes ci'adas chirp deep at night.
Sweet smell of ricefields shows a bumper year,
A surge of frogs' croaks to the ear.

Seven or eight stars beyond clouds in th' sky,
Two or three raindrops b'fore hills high.
The old thatched inn beside trees of the fane,
Hut in sight, across th' bridge winds th' lane.

菩萨蛮·书江西造口壁

辛弃疾

郁孤台下清江水，
中间多少行人泪。
西北望长安，
可怜无数山。

青山遮不住，
毕竟东流去。
江晚正愁余，
山深闻鹧鸪。

The Buddha Envoy·
Writing on the Wall of Zaokou, Jiangxi

Xin Qiji

Below th' Gloom Terrace is th' Clear River flow;

In it, how many passers-by's tears go?

I look far to Xi'an northwest;

A shame's that countless mountains rest.

Green mountains can't block th' water flow;

After all eastward it does go.

Woe the river of dusk does bring,

Mountains deep, th' partridge heard to sing.

醉太平

刘　过

情高意真，
眉长鬓青。
小楼明月调筝，
写春风数声。

思君忆君，
魂牵梦萦。
翠销香暖云屏，
更那堪酒醒！

Drunk in Peace

Liu Guo

Heart true, high mind to bear,
Brows long with black side hair,
In th' moonlit tower zither strings I pluck,
A tune played like the mild spring air.

I miss you, all of thine;
You haunt mind 'nd dream of mine.
Th' blue hue gone, warm incense dims the cloud screen,
Let alone when I'm clear from wine.

浣溪沙

姜　夔

著酒行行满袂风。
草枯霜鹘落晴空。
销魂都在夕阳中。

恨入四弦人欲老，
梦寻千驿意难通。
当时何似莫匆匆。

Yarn Washing

Jiang Kui

Tipsy, sleeves filled with breeze, roam I;
Grass sere, falcons down from th' bright sky.
In the setting sun woe does lie.

Grief in my four strings has aged me;
Dream-search far, th' shared mind hard to be,
Why should we part then hastily?

扬州慢

姜 夔

淮左名都，

竹西佳处，

解鞍少驻初程。

过春风十里，

尽荠麦青青。

自胡马窥江去后，

废池乔木，

犹厌言兵。

渐黄昏，

清角吹寒，

都在空城。

杜郎俊赏，

算而今、重到须惊。

纵豆蔻词工，

青楼梦好，

难赋深情。

二十四桥仍在，

波心荡、

冷月无声。

念桥边红药，

年年知为谁生。

Song of Slow Yangzhou

Jiang Kui

At th' famed town east of the River,
At th' scenic spot of Bamboo West,
I let the saddle down for a short stay.
I go in spring wind on the ten-mile way.
All around are wheat and weed green.
Since across the river Jin steeds have been,
Tall trees and pools they tore
Have been tired of the war.
Dusk to draw near,
Cold blow horns clear,
All in the void town drear.

The place Du Mu has prized,
If he comes today, must make him surprised.
Despite his gift for diction schemes
And his sweet brothel dreams,
His woe can't be expressed.
The Twenty-four Bridge still does rest;
The ripples have rolled;
In quietness is th' moon cold.
As for the Chinese peonies red,
From year to year whose life they've led!

月上瓜洲·南徐多景楼作

张 辑

江头又见新秋，
几多愁？
塞草连天，
何处是神州？

英雄恨，
古今泪，
水东流。
惟有渔竿明月，
上瓜洲。

The Moon over Guazhou·
Written at the Multi-view Tower

Zhang Ji

The riverside has met autumn again:
How much woe then?
Frontier grass vast to th' sky,
Where on earth does th' Divine Land lie?

Heroes' woe 'nd tear
Of th'past 'nd this year
East with streams flow.
With the fishing line and moon glow,
To th' isle I go.

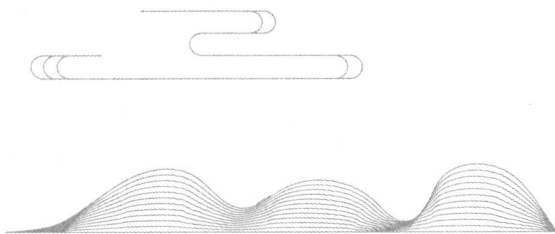

卜算子

游次公

风雨送人来，
风雨留人住。
草草杯盘话别离，
风雨催人去。

泪眼不曾晴，
眉黛愁还聚。
明日相思莫上楼，
楼上多风雨。

Divination

You Cigong

Wind and rain witness you come nigh;
Wind and rain bring you to a stay.
In haste with cups and dishes we say bye;
Wind and rain hurry you away.

Your tearful eyes have not been dry;
Your eyebrows are knitted for woe.
Lovesick under the moon, don't climb upstairs;
Through the upstairs wind and rain go.

一剪梅·舟过吴江

蒋 捷

一片春愁待酒浇。

江上舟摇。

楼上帘招。

秋娘渡与泰娘桥。

风又飘飘。

雨又潇潇。

何日归家洗客袍。

银字笙调。

心字香烧。

流光容易把人抛。

红了樱桃。

绿了芭蕉。

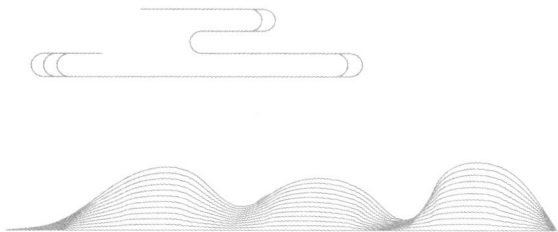

A Spray of Plum Blossoms·
My Boat Passing the Wu River

Jiang Jie

A surge of spring woe to be drowned in wine,
On th' River sways my boat;
Flutters the wineshop sign.
The Qiuniang Ferry 'nd the Tainiang Bridge float,
In wind that blows again,
In rain that falls again.

To wash my robe, home when can I return?
Th' sil'er-inlayed flute to tune,
Th' heart-shaped incense to burn.
Time 'nd tide are prone to throw man behind soon:
Red cherries are let grow,
Green bananas let grow.

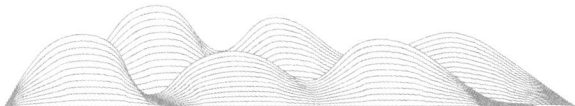

虞美人·听雨

蒋 捷

少年听雨歌楼上，
红烛昏罗帐。
壮年听雨客舟中。
江阔云低，
断雁叫西风。

而今听雨僧庐下，
鬓已星星也。
悲欢离合总无情。
一任阶前，
点滴到天明。

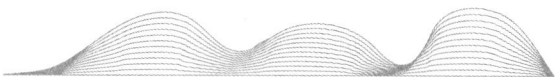

Beautiful Lady Yu·Listening to Rain

Jiang Jie

He listens to rain in th' songhouse, th' young guy,
Candles red with dim curtained bed.
He listens to rain in th' boat, th' adult guy.
Th' river vast, low clouds spread;
In th' breeze a lost wild goose does cry.

Now he listens to rain at the fane's eave,
With grey hair temples are inset.
It's cruel to part, unite, rejoice or grieve,
Rain in front of th' steps let
Till break of day drop and not leave.

·参考文献·

［1］Paloposki, Outi, & Kaisa. Koskinen. A Thousand and One Translation: Revisiting Retranslation［M］// G. Hansen, K. Malmkjaer, and D. Gile (Eds.). *Claims, Changes, and Challenges in Translation Studies*. Amsterdam: Benjamins, 2004: 27–38.

［2］（法）程抱一,著. 中国诗歌语言研究［M］. 涂卫群,译. 北京:商务印书馆,2023.

［3］北京大学古文献研究所,编. 全宋诗［M］. 北京:北京大学出版社,1992.

［4］钱锺书,集. 宋诗选注［M］. 北京:生活•读书•新知三联书店,2002.

［5］唐圭璋,编纂. 全宋词(简体增订本)［M］. 王仲闻,参订. 孔凡礼,补辑. 北京:中华书局,1999.

［6］唐圭璋,笺注. 宋词三百首笺注［M］. 北京:人民文学出版社,2005.

［7］王国维,著. 人间词话［M］. 范雅,编著. 南京:江苏人民出版社,2016.

［8］王力,著. 王力谈诗词格律［M］. 南京:江苏人民出版社,2019.

［9］吴战垒,著. 中国诗学［M］. 上海:东方出版社,2021.

［10］许渊冲,译. 宋词三百首［M］. 北京:五洲传播出版社,2012.

［11］赵彦春,译. 英韵唐诗百首［M］. 北京:高等教育出版社,2019.

［12］朱光潜,著. 诗论［M］. 上海:华东师范大学出版社,2018.

［13］朱孝臧,选编. 宋词三百首［M］. 王宏义,注译. 贵阳:孔学堂书局,2019.